"What a perfect servant you are," he taunted

Suddenly the seat of the Bentley was too small for both of them. She wished he hadn't chosen to sit in front with her. "Thank you, sir," was all she said.

Ivan smiled mockingly. "Does nothing get you mad?"

"Not much, sir. Nothing you would know about."

"Stop here," he said. "We're going to talk."

Fear gathered in Rachel's stomach. It was the early hours of the morning and the street was deserted. She pulled over and cut the engine. She knew what was coming, and she mustn't allow it.

SARA WOOD lives in a rambling sixteenth-century home in the medieval town of Lewes amid the Sussex hills. Her sons have claimed the cellar for bikes, making ferret cages, taxidermy and winemaking, while Sara has virtually taken over the study with her reference books, word processor and what have you. Her amiable, tolerant husband, she says, squeezes in wherever he finds room. After having tried many careers—secretary, guest-house proprietor, play-group owner and primary teacher—she now finds writing romance novels gives her enormous pleasure.

Books by Sara Wood

SARA WOOD

savage hunger

Harlequin Books

TORONTO • NEW YORK • LONDON
AMSTERDAM • PARIS • SYDNEY • HAMBURG
STOCKHOLM • ATHENS • TOKYO • MILAN

Harlequin Presents first edition December 1988
ISBN 0-373-11134-7

Original hardcover edition published in 1988
by Mills & Boon Limited

CHAPTER ONE

WITH her face set in its habitually earnest expression, Rachel searched the carriage until she found privacy. A brief shrug disposed of the severely tailored jacket, revealing a far from childlike body, the sensual swell of her breasts and hips quite at odds with her clothes and demeanour. She placed her hands under her rear, smoothing out the grey flannel skirt as she sat down, so that it would still be immaculate when she arrived.

The train jerked protestingly out of the station. As it gathered speed, Rachel stared longingly at the water meadows, hazy from heavy dew. She'd much rather be togged up in dungarees and wellington boots, striding across those fields, instead of imprisoned in tight clothes and inflexible court shoes.

Rich brown fields flashed by, disappearing with ghostly trees into the autumn mist. There was a mysterious, magical world beyond those trees, and she wished she could abandon her journey and seek it out. The lure of freedom was overwhelmingly tempting. Somewhere lurked romance in the guise of a gentle, fair-haired man who was kind, considerate and deeply loving. He had to be fair. That early passion for dark men had been very thoroughly laid to rest.

Thick brown lashes hid the wistful look that had flickered into her nut-brown eyes, as common sense took over from wishful thinking. Financial security and independence were her priorities. She must be sensible.

Iván Lutero Posada represented security—or, at least, potential security. Maybe he was granting her an interview out of curiosity, but at least it gave her a chance to land the job. Carefully, Rachel removed the map of London from her bag and went over the route again. There were plenty of buses from Victoria Station to Westminster Bridge; then a short walk along the Embankment to King's Reach, wave the magic security pass, and let the best man win. Woman. Unless... Her soft eyes became troubled. Unless he was a chauvinist.

Enticing hedgerows, tumbling with glossy berries, zipped by unnoticed. Her lack of finance was the cause for the frequent biting of her lower lip, and the small frown that marred her clear brow. She had precisely eight pounds twenty in the bank, perfect health, an ability to cook and drive, and the knowledge that she was plain and nondescript. She'd learnt *that* fact early in her life.

All Rachel knew of her background was that she'd been abandoned by her mother in a waiting-room at Guy's Hospital. It was some time before anyone discovered the quiet, placid baby. Then she had become one of London's waifs and strays, spending her childhood years in a variety of institutions and foster homes, often ignored, sometimes neglected.

No one had ever praised her in any way at all. Even her ex-husband had claimed it was her body that attracted him. She knew it had been a mistake to throw caution to the winds and wear that uncharacteristically sexy dress to the office party—so much for taking advice from a flatmate! A love-starved Rachel had mistaken the darkly attractive Alan's lust for love. The fact that she refused him her body had only whetted his appetite, and her eager, innocent pleasure from his practised compliments had excited him to rashness. Their hasty marriage had proved to be a disaster.

Alan had consoled himself in reckless spending, while she worked desperately hard to increase their income and create the home she'd never had. So hard that her tiredness gave her the excuse she needed to avoid her husband's unsatisfactory lovemaking, and Alan began to look elsewhere for his pleasures.

Rachel shuddered as she recalled discovering that she'd been betrayed. So many times in her life she'd tried to give her love, only to have it trampled on. Once again, she retreated into her shell, the calm barrier of reserve thicker now, burying deep emotions and passion. She kept life at a distance, knowing that was the only safe method of protection from deep hurt. Life had dealt her so many blows in the past and, until she was emotionally stronger, she had no intention of risking any more.

Two stops before Victoria, Rachel composed her thoughts and checked her appearance. It wasn't necessary to tidy her hair—the smooth brown silk had been neatly parted down the centre of her head and drawn in shining curves over her ears to tuck into a firm French pleat. To look at the governess-style simplicity, no one would know what long rich tresses flowed down her back when she released the pleat at bedtime. She examined her face critically, giving the plain, straight nose a dash of powder and the unsmiling mouth a slick of pink lipstick, since most of it had been chewed away. The big brown eyes stared at her solemnly from under their heavy fringe of lashes—her only vanity. She'd do.

She found the apartment block at King's Reach and pushed her way into a very modern and spacious entrance hall, which seemed to be masquerading as a jungle. Some of the plants couldn't possibly be real, they were far too exotic!

'You have a pass, miss?' A uniformed Tarzan blocked her way.

'Pass? Oh, yes.' Suppressing a smile, she snapped open her handbag—how she hated handbags!—and took out the gold-crowned security card, half expecting the man to say, 'Pass, Friend.'

'Thank you, miss.' He read the flamboyant scrawl on the card. 'Mr Posada has the Garden Terrace suite. That door there.'

Rachel crossed the marble-tiled floor, feeling very self-conscious as her heels clacked noisily, and even sillier trying to walk quietly. Although she couldn't actually see him, she knew that Tarzan's eyes were following her. She rang the bell by the mahogany door.

'Yes?'

The abrupt voice from the small grille above the bell made her jump. She hated those things. You never knew how close to get to them: whether to shout or whisper.

'Good morning. I'm Rachel Wells. I have an appointment to...'

'Come in.'

The door opened magically. Formal set-ups intimidated Rachel dreadfully, especially when those disembodied voices were as curt and unwelcoming as this one had been. Hesitantly, she pushed open an inner door and found herself the subject of surprised attention from four very well groomed men in neat, dark suits.

'Well! This is a turn up for the books. You're not after the job, are you?' asked one.

'Yes, I am,' she said calmly.

'Jeez! You women get everywhere!'

Her serious gaze assessed him. 'I was about to say the same thing about you men,' she said drily. 'Are you all waiting to be interviewed?'

'Yup. One in there at the moment. He's seeing us in order of arrival, so you're last.' He jerked a shiny head of hair towards a door at the end of the large sitting-room and Rachel began to take in her surroundings as she sank into an easy chair, relieved that she had a while to compose herself.

After their initial surprise, the men ignored her, chattering to each other about their present employers and swapping scandalous stories. Rachel was used to being disregarded and used the time profitably, going over the questions she expected.

The door at the end opened. A tall blond man walked smartly into the sitting-room, but immediately the door closed behind him, his shoulders slumped and he passed a weary hand over his forehead.

'What's he like?' asked one of the men.

This wasn't the prospective employer, then—Rachel had hoped it was, he looked rather nice.

'What would you expect from a man who earns his living tearing people apart? He's an out and out bastard,' he said bitterly. 'I feel like I've been interrogated by MI5. If you've got any sense, you'll cut your losses and join me in the pub. I need a stiff drink.'

A stocky Scot rapped sharply on the door of the tiger's lair and disappeared inside to be gobbled up and spat out. Rachel's forehead crinkled in worry, then cleared. This could be to her advantage. These men might be too proud to work for a difficult employer, whereas she was too hard up to be proud, and her upbringing had taught her how to bite her tongue, be polite and hide her feelings. Still, it would have helped if she'd asked what kind of a bastard Mr Posada was.

He was a rich one, that was clear. The apartment stood in a prime part of the Thames riverbank, within sight of the Houses of Parliament. Glass formed the entire river side of the room, and through it she could see a large terrace, dotted with rattan chairs and tables under a royal blue and white striped awning, shielding them from the October sun. Embryo saplings and ornamental-leaved plants had been planted in artistic groups around the terrace, offering tantalising glimpses of the river beyond.

The sitting-room was less appealing. It had no character, for one thing. Ethereal white drapes framed the windows, a white, ankle-spraining carpet deadened sound and pale eau-de-Nil walls gleamed, pristine and impersonal. A few tasteful sculptures in steel arced and clawed across low glass tables, and two silver-leafed trees bent their weeping branches to the ground. No one could form an opinion of the occupant from the room—there was a complete absence of clues and certainly none to indicate he was half-Colombian, a fact she'd picked up in the gossip columns. The only comfortable things in the room were the chairs. They looked untouchable, upholstered in silver thread and framed by steel tubing, but were perfectly shaped to the body and Rachel coveted them.

Raised voices heralded the exit of the stocky Scot, who merely lifted his eyebrows expressively at the next man, shrugged and slammed the door on the way out.

By the time it was Rachel's turn, she was extremely apprehensive. None of the men had looked pleased after their interviews. She picked up her bag, straightened her jacket and moved quietly across the room, breathing deeply for control. Experience, perfect poise, a retiring manner, self-effacement and clean fingernails: what more could he want?

But the poise was shattered the moment she walked in. Iván Lutero Posada stunned her into immobility at first sight, and this was an effect she later noticed time and time again. Few stayed immune to the impact of the incredible vitality that poured untiringly from his body, or escaped a small *frisson* of danger at the intense sensation of carefully controlled, deliberately projected violence. The room positively hummed with his dark, intimidating presence. She saw little else but his dominating will, which drew everything inexorably into the dark cavern of his mind and body, as if he embodied hell itself. In the subdued lighting, he gave the impression of a man who was as hard and impenetrable as jet. His Colombian blood was never more apparent than when he brooded—which, she discovered, was often—and he was brooding now, sitting casually on the edge of his desk, one long, elegant leg swinging in deceptive negligence, searing her with fierce black eyes. In that relaxed position, he oughtn't to have looked threatening and tense, but he did. Even asleep he probably had that half-watchful look, ready to strike or silently withdraw with equal rapidity.

He was around thirty-six and his face was world-weary. As a political cartoonist and satirist, he was a national figure. As a rake in the public spotlight, he had provided reporters with plenty of material for salacious stories. All the carnal urges of mankind were contained in his expression, and a hard, jaded cynicism lurked in his eyes.

'I'm fresh out of megaphones.'

His voice was a shock, the softest black velvet, subtly cloaking an underlying sneer. It made her strain forwards to catch what he said, and watch him intently to half read his lips. Rachel wondered whether this was an intentional ploy to put people at a disadvantage. She decided it was. This man knew exactly what he was doing, twenty-four hours of the day. There was a ruthless, calculating air about him and she was certain that he fully intended to be intimidating.

'Closer,' he drawled, when she didn't appear to understand his cryptic remark. 'I find it difficult to interview people half a mile away.'

'Oh, of course, sorry.' Rachel blinked and lowered her eyes, taking up the chair he had indicated with a briefly pointed finger. She kept her eyes down to avoid meeting his. They had a nasty stare of laser-beam quality, hunting out all her weaknesses and foibles, penetrating into her very soul. At least, that was what it seemed like. It was probably a technique he'd learned while stalking politicians and opening up their mouths and brains with a surgeon's precision.

Molten lava flowed in his voice. 'How do you do, Mrs Wells? I am Iván Posada.' He extended his hand.

Ee-*varn*, he'd pronounced it, she registered. She forced a polite greeting and firmly grasped the lean brown fingers, trying not to recoil from the electrifying sensation that accompanied his handshake.

'Relax.'

Not a man to waste words, she thought, unless of course they were lethal indictments of politicians. 'Thank you, I will.' She gave him a pleasant but remote smile. If he was going to act the curt interviewer, she'd play the charming, unruffled interviewee. This could be quite fun!

Very carefully, she crossed her legs primly at the ankles and placed her hands neatly in her lap. A quickly flicked glance confirmed that he'd found her response amusing, but then, to her consternation, his eyes ran all over her body, examining it intently. He began with the plain black court shoes—were they still highly polished? She resisted the urge to check. Next under his scrutiny came her long, slender legs, pressed firmly together. His eyes swerved around her curving hips, dipping into the waist of the fitted jacket, following the plush fullness that betrayed the presence of her breasts.

His detailed appraisal was raising the hairs on the back of her neck. It was only a test, to disconcert her, of course. Her training had included mock interviews like this. This man's perception of her role was obvious, and she had to struggle with the immediate sensation of inferiority and subjugation that his glance had aroused in her.

The dark eyes scanned her face, noticing everything and, much against her will, she was forced to look at him. God, he was handsome! Unfairly, devastatingly so. Perfectly groomed, blue-black hair slicked back from a widow's peak, a tanned, strong-boned face so smooth that it seemed no hair would dare grow on it apart from the neat black sideburns that angled into the hollow of his cheek. His nose was strong and manly, its perfection spoiled by the fact that someone had once smashed his face with a fist, so driven by violence that the bone had broken, adding menace to his already threatening features. Either the same man, or another, had split one of his extraordinarily high Latin American cheekbones, because a faint scar dented its prominence. His mouth had been hacked out of granite and defined by cynical creases which indicated the habitual sarcasm that shaped it. Combined with the wide shoulders and deep chest, clad in a fine black pin-stripe that tapered to lean hips and long legs, the overall impression was one of immense power and dynamic energy. A man's man. The kind of man who not only didn't eat quiche, but had probably never heard of it; who might open doors for women and stand them dinner, but would expect them to pay with their bodies afterwards. For why would anyone expect anything else of such a rawly sensual animal?

'Tell me——' Iván reached over to a file, extracting her letter and curriculum vitae with a long slender hand, laying them side by side so that he could see them clearly. Enough vitriol had dripped from those fingers into his pen to annihilate half the politicians in the House. 'Why on earth should I employ a woman?'

'That's for you to judge, Mr Posada. I don't know the qualifications of my competitors. You do.' Was that too abrasive? She said it quite pleasantly, hard though that had been in response to his taunt.

'You're very young. Twenty-three.' He was frowning.

'Yes. About the same age as the other candidates.' Her tone was remarkably level.

'They didn't get the job,' he observed drily.

'I'm mature and experienced enough.'

An eyebrow lifted fractionally at the word 'experienced,' but Rachel held his gaze stoically, not rising to his suggestive expression. 'And what has given you this maturity, would you say?' he murmured.

'A tough life.' She was conscious that he had become very still, as if he had suspended the process of breathing. He could assume the most perfect poker face that she'd ever seen! 'I—I was fostered,' she said with unusual frankness. What on earth had possessed her? Those darn tongue-loosening eyes of his. They had narrowed to slits and she wished she hadn't begun to tell him, but carried on resolutely. She'd started, so she'd finish and to hell with him. 'I had a number of homes and learnt to be self-sufficient at an early age, and not rely on other people for anything.'

'Why were you fostered?'

'Is that relevant?' she asked coldly.

'It could be. Any reason why you shouldn't tell me?'

'No. I was illegitimate. My mother didn't want me.' Despite her intentions, a small tremor hovered in her voice. It still hurt. No one had ever loved her for long.

'Then we have something in common, Mrs Wells,' he said softly, and she looked up, her big brown eyes moist and startled. 'I was illegitimate, and my father didn't want me enough to disrupt his life.'

Rachel found herself falling into his dark, bottomless eyes, and imagined that she saw first sadness and then bitterness there before she averted her head, confused. She seemed to have struck a human chord within him. Perhaps his hard exterior hid a great deal of pain and hurt, just like hers. A warm empathy gentled the solemn lines of her face.

'Hmm.' His relentless gaze stripped her brain methodically till she was sure he could see all her past, laid out in its sordid, miserable muddle. 'What masochistic tendencies make you pine to spend your days in traffic jams, raising your blood pressure, inhaling lead fumes and carbon monoxide?'

The moment had gone. Her impression of a sensitive man had been in her own imagination, and was swept away by the cynical black glint in his eyes and the sour twist to his mouth. He was back to his original softly spoken, yet biting manner. Rachel was beginning to tune in to this curt, unorthodox approach. 'Hunger, Mr Posada. That and a lack of other skills.'

'You're a little slow on the uptake, Mrs Wells. Are you always bad at summing up people? I don't fall for sob stories. I missed out when the good fairy godmother dished out humane qualities like pity,' he said in his smooth, brandy voice. Like brandy, it had a hidden kick. 'All I got was a violent initiation by the wicked fairy. Try another tack.'

'I was merely stating the facts.' She refrained from saying that it was perfectly obvious he didn't have one shred of pity in the whole of his body. If he did, he would be more conscious of an interviewee's nerves. 'You asked me why I was insane enough to want to be your chauffeur, and I told you the reasons.'

He slid from the desk and just looked at her for a long time. 'I'm not quite sure whether you are choosing your words cleverly, and are taking the mickey out of me, or whether you are sublimely innocent.'

Rachel smiled to herself and was subjected to further intense scrutiny, the dark, penetrating eyes alive with a wry humour.

'Wells Fargo can't fault your driving.'

His words startled her. The company had belonged to Alan, her ex-husband, and he had refused to give her any references from his express mail and chauffeur service after she'd humiliated his mistress. How had Iván Posada got any information about her? Typically, he seemed to know what she was wondering.

'Some of the secretaries at Fargo have big mouths after a few drinks,' explained Iván, with a mocking smile.

'I see,' she said calmly. It was just as well she had nothing to hide. After four years of driving around London, chauffeuring anything from pop stars to Bolivian attachés and African masks to rare blood, her record was perfect. There had been nothing and no one lost, no trouble, plenty of drama soothed by her reserves of calm patience and common sense.

Yet she hated his sneaky investigation. 'It would have been simpler and cheaper to give me a test run instead. Oh!' She put her hand to her mouth, realising what she'd just said.

A grin, characterised by brilliant white teeth against dark skin, chased briefly across his face. 'What an interesting idea,' Iván murmured.

He assessed Rachel thoughtfully, then drew a chair up in front of her. He leaned back, casually resting one leg on his knee, grasping his ankle with tanned fingers. Rachel's eyes were drawn to the taut material stretching over the muscles in his thigh that had expanded with the movement, and she passed a nervous tongue over dry lips. The man oozed sensuality from every pore.

'Bastard, was he?'

His mind did jump about! Rachel tried to look detached. 'If you mean my late employer, my ex-husband, it was just a case of incompatibility.'

'Well, well,' he drawled. 'A miracle. A woman who isn't vindictive.'

She wondered what kind of women he knew to make that kind of a remark. She felt vaguely sorry for him. He'd be bound to attract the wrong sort. No nice girl would give him a chance to get near her!

'What's wrong with the job you've got?' he asked silkily.

'Agency work is uncertain, and I need a steady income. I've only been on their books a few months, and preference goes to long-term drivers. Being near Gatwick is handy, but the best work is in London.' She didn't add that her basement flat was cold, damp and unwelcoming. He wouldn't care.

Iván rose with a lithe uncoiling of his body, and began to pace up and down. 'It's the rush hour. I'm late for a meeting, we're in the middle of Oxford Street and the car breaks down. What do you do first?'

'Reassure you.'

He bit back an exclamation of surprise, which secretly pleased Rachel. He wasn't going to be the only one in this interview with unusual angles on life!

'Always supposing I need it, and don't fire you for insolence, what then?' he asked with hooded eyes.

'It would depend on how far it was to your destination. It might be within walking distance.'

'It's raining. I've recently had pneumonia and the doctor has forbidden me to walk in the rain.'

Controlling a smile, Rachel considered her reply, longing to tell him that no one had ever looked fitter than he, and it was unlikely that he'd ever allow anyone to forbid him to do anything.

'I see. I could help you on to a bus or show you which tube to take,' she said, hoping he noticed that her words might indicate a mother shepherding a child.

'My destination is not on a tube route and all the buses are crammed full with pregnant schoolgirls.'

She grinned. They would be. 'I'd try for a taxi.'

'There aren't any.'

'In that case, I'd make sure you were comfortable and had something to amuse yourself with and roll up my sleeves. I took a course in mechanics, Mr Posada, at the Chauffeur Training School.' His eyes had twinkled momentarily when she had patronised him with the word 'amuse'. Rachel decided there was something redeemable about this extraordinary man, if he could laugh at a put-down like that.

'I know. But this is a breakdown you can't remedy,' he continued relentlessly.

'Since I would have been maintaining the car, that's not very likely,' she said, calmly but firmly. 'However, if that is the case then there's nothing either of us can do but telephone and delay the appointment.'

'All the telephone boxes in a radius of two miles have been vandalised and every shop is closed.'

'But,' purred Rachel triumphantly, 'we'd be ringing from your car telephone.'

'I don't have one,' he said softly.

'*Really?* I'm astounded. May I recommend that you do?' she said sweetly. 'For a man like you, it would be invaluable.'

His glare burnt away a few more brain cells. 'What, precisely, is a man like me?'

'Precisely? An extremely busy and impatient one, always in a hurry,' she said, quite composed.

His mouth compressed as he sauntered out of her sight. When he spoke again, she realised he was standing immediately behind her chair. Another interview technique she'd learnt. The trick was to pretend he was in front of you and continue the conversation as normally as possible.

'What was your percentage in the mechanics exam?'

'They award grades, Mr Posada—perhaps you'd forgotten for a moment—and I had an A grade.' He was testing the truth of her claim that she'd attended the course. 'I didn't like to bring my certificates, that would have seemed like boasting.' She had won entry to the school in a competition at the age of eighteen, and walked straight into a job with Wells Fargo. And marriage to Alan.

'Your lover asks you to dinner with his family. You know it is a step towards a proposal. I ask you to collect someone from Heathrow. What do you do?'

'Drive to Heathrow,' she answered promptly. 'The conflict wouldn't arise, you see. I have no attachments of any kind, and intend to keep it that way.'

To Rachel's relief, the telephone rang, burring softly, as sensuous and sinister as Iván himself. With a quick murmur of polite apology—habit rather than deeply felt, she decided—he strode to the desk and lifted the receiver. Rachel was released from the high-octane scrutiny as his power was transferred to the caller.

It was extraordinary, but she had been concentrating so intently on the man that the room had made no conscious impression on her senses. This was obviously his study. Beyond the cluttered desk was a large drawing-board, angled to get the best light. Pots of felt-tips, pencils, brushes and inks lay scattered on the deep windowsill, and huge sheets of stiff cartridge paper had been stacked in the corner. This was a much better indication of his personality. Rachel could imagine those papers and paints being thrown around in private, violent rages. Certainly the desk looked as though he'd made savage forays on it, searching for documents and articles. Did his employees suffer from his rages, or were they strictly secret? Iván Posada gave her the appearance of a man who liked to keep control of himself—unless it suited him.

Lining three walls of the room, reference books jostled for shelf space with copies of the magazines Iván had worked on. He'd just been snapped up by *In Sight*, the wicked satirical glossy that competed with the magazine he'd recently left in New York.

Her soft eyes considered him. Did she really want to work for a man like this? Did a penniless woman have any choice? She had to get a decent job soon. It was becoming impossible to afford even the essentials. Perhaps she'd been a fool to walk out on Alan and proudly refuse any maintenance. But she hadn't wanted anything that had been connected with him; no furniture, equipment, and especially no money. She wanted to forget that she'd ever been married. Anything, even working for a quick-tempered, sexy rat, was better than living with Alan. At least she wouldn't be humiliated every day of her life.

Now she wasn't in the path of Iván's searing stare, she was able to examine him a little more thoroughly. He stood arrogantly, with his legs apart, still dominating the room with his extraordinary potency. His voice sounded like that of a husky kitten. No, forget that. Like a powerful black jaguar with its claws temporarily retracted. But the set of his muscular shoulders and the tensed sinews of his legs indicated a jaguar ready to leap and pounce in attack. He was always alert, always watchful.

A lean brown hand smoothed over the glossy black hair in an unhurried and oddly sensual gesture as it curved around his head to the nape of his neck, where the fingers absently stroked with a delicate touch. The line of his jet hair looked devastating against his tanned neck, and this in turn contrasted perfectly with the dazzling white starchiness of his shirt collar. This was an outward smoothie with a core of steel, or perhaps clashing knives, since there was a definite streak of cruelty in his nature. Even if she hadn't read some of his biting articles or winced at his pointed cartoons, she would have been aware of the lurking danger. Anyone who crossed him would get badly hurt.

'Samantha, believe me, nothing happened, only that kiss,' he was saying smoothly. 'You know how I am about redheads... No, don't do that. I like you as a blonde. Every last golden hair on your body,' he growled throatily.

Rachel raised her eyes to heaven. Surely women didn't actually swallow that sort of rubbish? It appeared they did. Samantha seemed to be appeased.

'Sure, tonight.' He gave a soft laugh at something the bedazzled Samantha said. 'Till seven.'

The receiver was replaced softly.

'How do you feel about drunks?'

'Pardon?'

Rachel was astonished. With barely a single break, he'd switched from being sexy and seductive to cold and efficient. Very impressive control. Better, even, than hers.

'One of the reasons I need a chauffeur is because I eat out frequently—business lunches, with plenty of liquid refreshment for my prey. I get them cheerful, Mrs

Wells. They talk more freely that way. Sometimes I feel honour bound to see them safely home or to their clubs.'

Rachel doubted that he had any honour. She knew the people he dealt with couldn't exactly be considered the nice boy-next-door type, but his ethics were still a bit questionable.

'And me,' he said, pushing his hands in his pockets. Her eyes were drawn to the lean thighs, and something unnervingly like a tiny trickle of arousal crept inside her body. 'I become a little reckless sometimes, too, after a few whiskies. Think you can cope with an uninhibited male?' His eyes gleamed with mischief.

He was taunting her deliberately, to see how she'd react if he became amorous. There it was again. An unmistakable quiver of pleasure.

'Uninhibited males are usually little boys under the surface,' she said in her best matter-of-fact tone, and was rewarded by his soft chuckle. 'Men tend not to proposition me or cause trouble. They seem to know that I don't find them in the least bit intimidating, threatening or sexually attractive.' She hoped he'd get the message.

But no man had raked her with his eyes so slowly and so sensuously before. From the way his expression mocked her, he would rather like to prove her words wrong. It was just the sort of thing that would amuse him.

'They always behave?' he asked, raising one dark brow in exaggerated amazement.

'Yes, Mr Posada. Always.' Despite her calm tone, she was nervous. Anyone would be, the way he stared. She crossed one leg over the other in a whisper of nylon and found his dark, brooding eyes running down the slender smoothness of her legs. His expression became suddenly sour.

'I have an uncommunicative daughter, a scheming sister and a lying brother,' he said with quiet savagery.

Rachel was stunned by his words. And surprised to hear that he was married, since the gossip columns only concentrated on destroying the reputations of the women he escorted, and constantly referred to the two occasions when he'd punched cameramen. But his condemning remarks about his family shed new light on him. Underneath that hard exterior was a callous interior.

'The job includes ferrying them around, too. There may be nauseous children with tireless and unceasing aspirations to wreck the car upholstery. How do you feel about that?'

'I've handled difficult children in my time, Mr Posada. I see no problem.' What a way to talk about your own child and her friends! He really was a hard brute.

'You like London?' he asked.

'Not particularly.'

'Do you prefer the country?'

Her face softened. 'Oh, yes.'

'Even farms oozing mud and stinking of dung?'

'I come complete with wellington boots,' she said, dead-pan.

'Sell yourself to me,' he snapped, sitting down and leaning forwards, capturing her with his eyes.

The man was relentless! 'I am not an object for sale, Mr Posada,' she said icily.

'No, I can see that,' he said, his expression unreadable. 'I apologise. My writing style tends to intrude into my life. Perhaps you'd tell me why you would make a good chauffeur. I know you can drive; would you care to summarise your other qualities?'

Despite his apology, Rachel had the distinct impression that he was still playing with her. She gave careful thought to her answer. 'I am quiet, capable and efficient,' she said. 'I don't flap, know London well, merge into the background but anticipate clients' needs. Like all good women drivers, I have no need to compete to show my skill. The safety and security of my client is the most important factor. I am neat, tidy, won't fill the car with heady perfume or check my lipstick in traffic jams. I don't wear aftershave, eat garlic or smoke a pipe, and I never forget to wash behind my ears.'

He smiled cynically. 'You sound perfect. Anything else? How about working antisocial hours?'

'I'm prepared to do that. I have no ties. It doesn't worry me at all.'

'Could you continue to be such a paragon even if I ignore you?' he murmured. 'Or like most women, would you expect constant praise and reassurance?'

Coming from any other man, the soft, sensual sound that issued from the granite-chipped mouth would have melted most women. But the tone and his words were so much at odds with each other, and held such an undercurrent of dislike for humanity—and women, in particular—that his very huskiness made her bones chill.

'Ignore me as much as you like. To be frank, I'd prefer that. I'm used to it. No one strokes my ego.'

'No, I don't suppose they do,' he agreed blandly.

Well, at least she knew where she stood! This man wasn't likely to lure her into his bed! After her initial attraction to his primitive call, she couldn't think why any woman would fancy the idea—it would be like mating with a ravening animal, with all that power-packed muscle and fierce, direct manner. No soft preliminaries there, no loveplay, no romance. Before her was a prime example of the tall, dark and handsome bastard, sexually and emotionally selfish. She gave a brief shudder.

'Cold, or nervous?'

'Neither.' He didn't miss anything.

There was a small, mirthless chuckle. 'I see.'

Hell, thought Rachel, that was a mistake. What did he see?

'I'll give you a try,' he said laconically.

Humble thanks, she grinned to herself, rejecting with regret the idea of a deep obeisance. 'That's most generous of you,' she said with widened eyes, and earning a mocking, knowing glance. He knew she was teasing him!

'Not at all,' he said. 'You're the first person who has responded to me with calm humour. I need people like that around me. My life is hard and fast. I need a driver to get me from A to B who won't grate on my nerves and doesn't take my preoccupation or anger personally. I get very wound up about deadlines and very irate about injustices.'

'Yes. I had picked up the impression that you didn't suffer fools gladly,' she said. So his manner had been an act, to some extent. Rachel brightened up at that, only to be disillusioned.

'Don't look so relieved,' he murmured. 'I'm not easy to work for. Your predecessor lasted two weeks. I suggest a probationary period for us both. Say four weeks. If I find I can't stand your amazing air of innocence and piety by then, you go. Although my family are sharing you, I'm the one who's paying you and I'm your boss. You obey me. Understand?'

'Perfectly, Mr Posada.'

'Start now. I need lunch. I'll explain your duties. They're a little complicated.'

Without waiting for her agreement, he strode towards the door. Rachel frowned in annoyance. She might have made some arrangements for lunch, but it had never occurred to him to ask. Pursing her lips at his high-handedness, she acknowledged that it would save her dipping into a boring tin of sardines at home. She was using him, not the other way around. She picked up her bag and followed, a little surprised that he was standing back for her to walk through the door first. In the underground car park, he handed over the keys and slid his long legs into the back.

The car was a Bentley Turbo: beautiful, sleek and shiny in dark maroon. It was a joy to drive. The engine was so quiet that she had to strain to hear it. But having him behind her made the back of her neck prickle and her palms sweat. It was like paddling gently in front of a hungry piranha. After flashing a quick glance in the driving mirror and finding his black brows drawn together in a lowering frown and his piercing eyes shafting shockingly into her innermost thoughts, she avoided locking glances with him again.

She dropped him at a restaurant in the West End and made for a little known parking spot, hurrying back and arriving quite breathless, unable to take time out to powder down the bright glow that illuminated her skin. Iván Lutero Posada would not wait for her. He'd probably be into his main course already.

In fact, he was just handing the menu to the moustachioed waiter when she appeared at the table, very much out of breath. It might have been her imagination, but she thought that his eyes had a soft, molten quality when he looked up at her across the red gingham tablecloth. Then his hooded lids concealed any expression, and the mask of neutrality descended as he stood courteously and waited until she had seated herself, before resuming his own seat.

'Sit down, Mrs Wells. I've ordered.'

She beckoned the waiter and held out her hand for the menu, studying it carefully while Iván let out a gentle chuckle. 'I'll have the avocado, followed by the sole and a side salad,' she said. There were one or two things her new boss needed to get straight, and the first was that she ran her own life.

'So, no change of order, sir,' said the waiter, bowing and making his exit.

Damn him for guessing so accurately! Iván was grinning his devil's grin, and Rachel wished she'd selected something weird just to annoy him. She hated being so predictable.

'Wine?' he murmured, with a wicked glance.

'No, thank you. I never drink if I'm driving.'

'Your qualities as a chauffeur far outweigh your qualities as an interesting woman. You must be the most boringly proper female I've ever met,' he observed.

'Thank you, Mr Posada.' Really, his comments went beyond the bounds of mere frankness!

The granite mouth curved at the corners. He took a long swallow of red wine, exposing a strongly corded and tanned neck. As Rachel traced the line of his carved jaw with her eyes, a small quiver disturbed her composure. It was so totally unexpected and unwelcome that she pushed her napkin on to the floor and spent a moment grovelling for it, in order to collect herself. It wasn't often, of course, that she sat a few feet away from one of the most handsome men in London. She was bound to quiver a bit. So long as he didn't notice; her pride would never allow that. It would make him laugh his designer socks off.

'For the next three weeks you'll be overpaid and underworked,' he said, his cynical mouth moist from the wine. Rachel watched, mesmerised, as the tip of his tongue briefly slid to the corner of his mouth. 'I spend quite a lot of time working at my apartment. You'll take me to the office occasionally, to lunch dates, the Houses of Parliament and so on. Please don't chatter. I use travelling time to begin composing my articles.'

'What about your daughter?' she asked.

'She doesn't live with me. My sister looks after her,' he said, almost biting off the words.

'Oh.' Rachel was puzzled at his evident anger, though it didn't appear to be directed at her, and she was intrigued by the arrangement. He broke in on her thoughts before she could speculate further.

'I'll explain all that in a moment. Let's get your duties in London sorted out. I'll expect you to work overtime, but you'll get the proper rate on top of your salary. Is that accepted?'

Since the salary was very generous, this was cherry on the cake to Rachel. Life was looking up. She nodded.

'I'm out to dinner every evening. There'll be the occasional visit to the theatre.' He jabbed a fierce fork into his cannelloni. 'I hope you read and can amuse yourself if there are lengthy curtain calls or whatever.'

'I can read,' she said drily. 'I'm way past the Ladybird primers.'

'Don't push me, Mrs Wells. My tongue is more acid than you can bear. Now, at the end of the three weeks, my sister and her husband will be bringing Anna—my daughter—back from holiday. You'll divide your time between London and the farm near Scaynes Hill where they live. My brother Tony's house.'

Was it her imagination, or did he sound bitter when he said that? Her fascinated eyes watched his teeth ripping savagely into a wholemeal roll. She pointedly broke hers into bite-size pieces and buttered each morsel with neat precision. He was smiling sardonically. He'd noticed her gesture.

'For reasons known only to themselves, my brother and sister don't drive. You'll be at their beck and call when my sister's husband isn't available, which is most of the time. His life revolves around castrating pigs, warble flies and grain yields.'

No one was safe from his nasty tongue. Rachel kept a non-committal expression on her face. 'Where will I live while I'm working in London?' she asked. 'The advertisement said it was a live-in job.'

'When you're not at the farm, you live with me. I need you on call. I have a room suitable for your needs.'

Probably the Black Hole of Calcutta, she mused. She watched his inscrutable face for a moment as he swept up the remnants of sauce with his roll. 'You have other staff?' she asked cautiously.

'No. I did, but they got in the way when I was working. You, I think, will not intrude. A woman comes in to clean for an hour each day, that's all. Apart from breakfast, I eat out. You can use the kitchen.'

Unobtrusive, unappealing, boring: that made her perfectly safe from his legendary rapacious appetites. Just as well he thought that. He was far too male to leave an attractive girl alone, and he wasn't the sort to have principles.

'Normally we'll spend weekends at the farm, and you'll be driving me to London early each Monday morning. I make all my heavy appointments at the beginning of the week. On Wednesday you'll return to the farm to do your share of the school rota and be on call for the rest of the family, then come and pick me up on Friday afternoon for the drive to Sussex. Do you want any pudding?'

'Er...no, thank you.'

'Go and get the car, then, while I have mine. You can take me to Cartiers.'

'Yes, Mr Posada.'

'Sir will do.'

Rachel raised her eyebrows fractionally.

'It will be easier for both of us,' he said, with a challenging look. 'Most of my contacts are pompous or pretentious. It helps to disconcert them. Besides, it will keep us at a distance, won't it?'

'Yes, sir,' she said calmly. It wouldn't hurt her, and he was right, it would keep them on a professional footing. On her training course she had been warned that employers might be on Christian name terms or expect a 'sir'. It was all part of the job. It wouldn't take her long to stash away enough money, then she could tell him to take a running jump. She'd had some difficult people to drive in her time, but this one had straight As in Unpleasantness. That vibrant, power-station of a personality hid a human glacier that flowed inexorably, grinding everything in its path and leaving scars. Still, there was no doubt that, if she could keep her cool and please him, it would give her enough confidence to work for anyone.

The Bentley whispered up to the kerb just as Iván stepped on to the pavement. Rachel leapt out and opened the car door, conscious that her boss was getting the eye from two passing beauties. He withered them with a single glance.

'Uniform,' he said, pausing, one hand on the door. She blinked at the unfathomable eyes, willing herself not to step back and show her dislike of being so close to him and the earthy sexiness that emanated from his body. 'Drop me at Cartiers and go along to Burlington Uniforms, Savile Row.' His eyes raked her body with offensive intimacy. 'Bottle-green. White shirt. Not double-breasted with a figure like that.' He bent his head and Rachel was sorely tempted to help him into the car with a well directed thrust from the toe of her shoe.

Instead she closed the door quietly and drove off into the lunch-time traffic.

What an unnerving man he was! This assignment looked like being a case of Mrs Nice versus Mr Nasty. Sweet Purity versus Sexy Satan. She smiled to herself at the vision of the battle between goodness and evil. This was going to be one humdinger of a job!

CHAPTER TWO

URGED on by her quiet sense of humour, Rachel calmly selected a beautiful sage-green suit at Burlington's. The joke was on Iván Posada: the soft, flowing lines which flattered her figure so successfully were the brainchild of an international designer and would cost him an arm and a leg.

'Take me home, Mrs Wells,' he said when she collected him in New Bond Street. 'Then you're free till tomorrow lunch time. Use the car to collect whatever you need to move in. Do you have much?'

'Virtually nothing,' she said, meeting his eyes in the mirror. Big mistake. Before she knew what she was doing, she was telling him her personal business. 'My ex-husband kept all the furniture and effects—I only took my own things with me when I moved.'

'Don't you ever stand up for your rights?' he enquired silkily.

'In my own way, sir,' she answered placidly.

'Doesn't sound like it. Tell me.'

Rachel considered. It might be a good idea—he'd be warned not to push her too far.

'I gathered up my husband's dirty washing and dropped it on his mistress's desk. She was his secretary, of course.'

A delighted, husky chuckle met her ears, and she grinned, too, at the memory. 'The next day I delivered the ironing,' she added, 'and one of his thermal vests that needed mending. I think it dented his macho image somewhat.'

'We all have secrets we hope no one will discover,' he murmured. 'I like your way, Mrs Wells. I must remember not to cross you.'

'Very wise, sir,' she said briskly, and that set him laughing again. It was a lovely sound, deep from his chest, bursting out uninhibitedly. She longed to see the difference it made to his face; how his eyes looked, his mouth, but although she knew he was watching her she kept her eyes stubbornly on the road. A charming Iván was more dangerous than an irascible one.

'So you have nothing of your own,' he said reflectively.

'I have myself. That's all I ever had and all I'm used to. I need no pity from anyone. What time shall I be ready for you tomorrow, sir?' she asked, anxious to get the conversation on to a more impersonal note. She never wanted to think about her marriage again. What was she doing, to have told him so much? It was totally unlike her.

'Twelve-thirty.' He leaned back, and Rachel felt the pressure on her brain recede.

It gave her enormous pleasure to change into dungarees and a roll-neck sweater and drive to her flat in the Bentley, which she packed with her mementoes, bric-a-brac and luggage. There wasn't much, and it didn't take long before she was back at King's Reach.

'Want any help, miss?'

Tarzan had seen her opening the boot, and the boxes in it. He came over to the car, his baby-blue eyes warm and friendly. It made a wonderful change from Iván's third degree approach. 'Thanks,' she grinned, handing him a couple of cases. Together they carted in her belongings and dumped them in the sitting-room.

The study door opened and Rachel felt unaccountably like a guilty schoolgirl, standing before a stern head teacher. Iván looked even more threatening and virile with his shirt-sleeves rolled up and buttons undone to the first few vigorous hairs on his chest.

'Who is on duty outside, Daniel?' he enquired with a slight frown.

'Er...me, sir,' replied the security man, blushing to the roots of his hair. Rachel felt he needed defending.

'My fault, Mr Posada,' she said, nervously twisting the strap of her dungarees. 'I enlisted his help.'

Iván was examining her outfit with bland interest. 'You should have called me. I'll see to this, Daniel. Some of the residents will give you hell if you're not at the door.'

'Sorry, Mr Posada.' Daniel dumped the cases and made an apologetic exit.

'Watch him,' said Iván silkily. 'He's a womaniser.'

With the distinct feeling that the pot was calling the kettle black, Rachel met his eyes squarely. 'I will watch him,' she said enthusiastically. He could try to fathom out her meaning, if he liked! Daniel was very watchable, a gorgeous hunk of man. Fair, too. She picked up a case and then stopped, confused, not knowing where to go.

'Put that down and I'll show you around.' Iván was reading her mind, as usual. 'You know the living-room and the study. They are my province, of course. The master bedroom is to our right, with access from the corridor and the study. Again, that won't interest you, will it?' His wicked eyes glittered at her.

'Not in the least,' she said emphatically.

His eyes flickered. 'Along this corridor here——' he flung open a pine-panelled door '—is the dining-room, which I rarely use unless I have caterers in for an office binge, and here...is the kitchen. As you can see, it's pretty large, and you can use it to eat in.'

'Oh, thank you.' That earned her a suspicious glance.

'Are you teasing me again?' he asked.

'I'm not sure,' she said earnestly.

A delighted laugh escaped from his lips. 'Careful, Mrs Wells. I might begin to like you, and that would be disastrous for both of us. Now here are the two spare bedrooms, not, I'm afraid, with river views like the rest of the rooms, but each has its own bathroom and is big enough to double up as a living-room for you. Choose whichever suits you best.'

Still trying to work out why liking her would be a problem, she peered into each one. Both were beautifully furnished, with a choice of pale beige or dusky blue colour schemes and she chose the latter. With a few of her possessions scattered around, it would cease looking so impersonal and take on a more homely air. Intending to settle in as soon as possible, she turned on her heel, only to bump into Iván, who had been standing directly behind her.

'Oh! Sorry!' she gasped.

His hands had steadied her briefly, and drawn her hard against his body in an instinctive reflex action that said a lot for his predatory habits. Rachel felt the burning imprint left by his fingers just before he pushed her away again with a soft hiss of breath.

It was the nearness of him, the incredible impact of being in contact with a few thousand volts of electric man, that made her incapable of action, and foolishly left her staring at him from under her thick fringe of sable lashes. The change in his features was so fundamental that she was left speechless. His sardonic mask had melted into sensual liquidity, proving that a very different man lurked under the cynical shellac. There was gentleness and longing, almost a mirror to her own deep desires, and therefore so shocking that Rachel could hardly breathe at the similarity of their needs. And the fact that he had allowed her to see a glimpse of his intensely passionate nature—and Rachel was sure it had been a conscious decision on his part—both worried and alarmed her.

'Clumsy of me . . . sir,' she breathed, remembering her position—and hoping that he would, too.

The word snapped him back, his mouth setting in grim lines as he collected her cases and dumped them in her room. They completed the move in silence, and Iván withdrew to the study. Rachel shut her own door and sat on the edge of the bed, a little stunned at his reaction—and hers. Could she have projected her own empty heart at him unconsciously, and accidentally discovered a sad, lonely man? Or was that tenderness she'd seen not his at all, but hers reflected? She'd never dared to trust her instincts before, they were too impulsive; and the idea of this dynamic man finding her not only attractive, but also appealing, was uncharacteristically arrogant on her part!

Yet she couldn't have imagined the sexual charge that fired them both. By all rights, Iván shouldn't be aroused by a plain mouse like her, but he was a man, and a hungry one at that. Well, now she was prepared; she wouldn't come into body contact with him again, or he might think she was giving him the go-ahead. It would be awful to get into a situation where she'd have to slap his face. That would mean an end to the job. Perhaps it had been just a test, to see whether she took up his challenge or not—she wouldn't put it past him. He was the most calculating and controlled man she'd ever met. Thank heavens the gullible Samantha was on the menu tonight!

He left by taxi, and Rachel never knew what time he returned. She woke after an untroubled, deep sleep, and snuggled happily into her pillow. The bed was unbelievably comfortable, and she felt very pampered to be living amid such luxury. The sheets and pillows were of the finest, soft powder-blue linen, delicately edged with navy lace. How the other half lived! A warm smile softened her serious face. In surroundings like these, she could cope with the wicked, woman-hopping Iván Posada.

The late autumn sun streamed in through a chink in the heavy damask curtains, sending a shaft of light over the floor. Languidly, she rolled over and slid her long silken legs to the edge of the bed, wriggling her toes delightedly in the thick, springy white carpet. After a quick shower, she emerged rosy-faced and glowing, giving her long tresses a hasty brush and slipping on a pair of briefs, stretch denim jeans and a white sweater.

Shoeless, she padded into the kitchen and stopped short, her eyes widening hugely.

Iván stood by the cooker, wearing nothing but a towel around his lean hips and, from the way he moved lithely towards her, it was in grave danger of falling away and revealing more than she was prepared to see.

'Good morning,' he husked, his eyes a dark velvet.

'Morning,' she managed, tearing her eyes away from his perfect, golden body, as unblemished as bronzed skin. An uncontrollable urge had risen within her to touch his skin, to brush it with her lips. What would it feel like? The thought skittered madly for a moment, making her blush, and then was dumped, fast. She began to slice some bread, concentrating hard. She would not think of the breadth of his shoulders, the brawny chest and the clusters of black glossy hairs. Nor would she allow the ripple that ran through her veins to unsettle her. He was too damn perfect. Rachel compressed her lips and viciously hacked at the loaf.

'Amazing how different a woman can look with her hair loose and tousled,' he said softly.

'That's a conclusion you've come to after years of research, I imagine,' she said tartly, angry that she wasn't looking prim and formal. It would have helped her to overcome this wanton response to him.

Rachel banged the bread in the toaster and poured herself a coffee from the percolator, aware that Iván was watching every move she made. She met his thoughtful gaze angrily.

'You mustn't believe gossip,' he said, stroking his broken nose with a long forefinger. 'My passions are too intense to be wasted on casual relationships.'

'Really?' She wasn't interested. She didn't want to hear about his passions. Already the intimacy of breakfast with a half-naked renegade was making her feel on edge.

In warning, she shot him a disapproving look. His mouth twisted wryly and he reached to a stack of newspapers, sliding one out and pushing the rest towards her.

She buttered her toast with slow, unhurried sweeps of the knife, then reached over to select her favourite newspaper. He must buy every one that was printed. Rachel's thick, gleaming mane slid silkily over her shoulder and hid her face from him as she munched away, finding it quite impossible to take in the lead story at all in Iván's electrifying presence.

He startled her by catching up her unending river of hair and pushing it away from her face. An index finger slowly came into vision to tuck a few of the sun-bronzed strands behind her small ear, and Rachel felt that indefinable surge that quickened her breathing. Drat him and his sensual hands!

'Forgive me, Mrs Wells, but I like to see people's faces,' he said quietly.

'Indeed.' Discomfited, she reached up and twisted her hair into a rope. Iván's eyes had strayed to her full breasts, which had lifted with the movement, and small hot darts of desire stabbed treacherously right into the centre of each peak. Shamed by her body's betrayal, she blushed again.

'Did you sleep well?' he asked throatily.

'Very well.'

'So the bed, at least, is to your liking. Do you think you'll stay, or is it too early to say?' He sounded amused.

'It all depends on you,' she answered, stony-faced.

'You mean...on whether I behave myself? Or whether I find you...satisfactory?'

Her stupid hands had become clammy with his husky tone, but she was filled with anger at his arrogance. 'On whether this remains a serious and professional relationship or not,' she said icily. She *wouldn't* repeat the mistake she made with Alan, falling for the man she worked for—she couldn't be such a fool! Couldn't she manage to work closely with a man without thinking he was Prince Charming? God, she must be longing for love and affection to be attracted to this carnal and openly sex-crazed man!

His sardonic mouth curved at her cold answer. 'That is perhaps the most respectful put-down I've ever had. However, if you expect me to treat you as an automaton when you're off-duty, perhaps you'd wear a bra. I find the pneumatic movement under that thin sweater just a little too much to bear at close quarters.'

His eyes dropped away, but not before licking her with a glance that made the blood in her body course into life. Rachel cursed him. She'd been a fool, thinking she was invisible to his eyes. He missed nothing. She ought to have known that Samantha wouldn't satisfy him for long. Sated and tired, he was still more alive than any man she'd ever known. 'I'll change now,' she said stiffly.

'No,' he growled, catching her arm. 'Finish your breakfast. I hate waste. Eat! And keep your hair neat in future.'

He was glaring at her ferociously. She made no reply, infuriated by his air of ownership. Instead, she primmed her face and lowered her eyes. He might also wear a bit more, she thought! He'd returned to scanning the papers. All the time, he was making notes and little sketches on a small pad beside him, planning the next crushing cartoon or acid-tipped thumbnail sketch of some unsuspecting politician's activities. Silently Rachel finished her breakfast and took her dishes to the sink.

'Dishwasher by your left thigh,' said Iván without glancing up.

Unreasonably irritated that not only did he know where her left thigh was but that he mentioned it as well, she found the catch on the door and stacked her crockery before making a deliberately unhurried exit.

Over the next few weeks a strangely ominous tension made an intangible link between them. Occasionally curt and brutally frank, he unnerved her by his unpredictability, but she tried to weather it with steady humour and understanding. His work sapped all his energy, leaving him little strength for social charm, and she accepted that.

His input was daunting. He'd rise at dawn to hear the early news and plan a topical cartoon, working through mealtimes to meet deadlines, accepting invitations to speak at dinners and often arriving back in the early hours. How he summoned up the physical strength to keep going, Rachel had no idea, but some demon pushed him, that was for sure. He had no contentment within, no calm, only an obsessive drive to pack as much into his waking hours as possible, and she felt a responsibility for this power-house of a man, who pushed himself too hard: a responsibility to provide a calm and sane environment.

In her spare time, she read his articles avidly. There were frequent exposés, satirical cartoons, pungent comments, all cutting through statements that smacked of lies and posturing. He wrote wickedly, denuding self-important people in the raw light of day. He was brilliantly clever with words and could slay anyone he chose. A little intimidated, Rachel vowed never to earn his anger.

Meeting his ribald colleagues on *In Sight* had been quite an experience. She was trying to fix herself something to eat when they all burst into the apartment unexpectedly, turning the kitchen into chaos as they heated up fish and chips.

'Kept damn quiet about your live-in lover, Daggers,' remarked an elegant elderly man.

Rachel met Iván's eyes with amusement. Daggers! What an appropriate name for him!

'I'm Mr Posada's chauffeur,' she said demurely, becoming immediately the centre of attention and much teasing.

'Stop, you ignorant hogs,' grinned Iván. 'You dare scare her off! She's a pearl among swine, and never more so than at this moment.'

More rude shouts, mocking Iván this time, then the elegant man addressed her again. 'My dear,' he said, 'if Daggers compliments you, then you are a rare woman indeed. First time I've ever heard him say anything nice about anybody. Have a chip.'

'Thank you,' said Rachel warmly.

So she'd stayed, occasionally weak with laughter at the repartee, occasionally acting as a judge between two—or three—angles on an article. But it was around Iván that the whole group spun, constantly referring to him, darting quick glances to see his response to their witticisms. As the afternoon wore on, and they refused to release her, Rachel became more and more aware of Iván's extraordinary magnetism. And her heart beat rapidly when she realised that he appeared to be performing for *her*. In the midst of all that madness and laughter, their eyes frequently met across the table, and it seemed there was a massive silence in the air. Iván's face would grow still, then she'd have to lower her lashes, unable to handle the intensity and meaning in his serious gaze.

She was emotionally ragged by the time they all disappeared around six o'clock, but managed to lose herself in an exciting TV film. He didn't return until dawn, and she rose at seven-thirty, wondering whether to wake him or not. In an hour they were going down to the farm, and Rachel was a little nervous at meeting his family.

She paused as she dressed in her uniform. He'd been nervous, too. Two days before, they'd spent a dreadful afternoon together in the toy shops, choosing presents for his daughter. Instead of being the fun that Rachel had expected, she'd found Iván's high-strung nerves difficult to cope with. It was as though he was afraid of displeasing Anna. Rachel spent a good deal of her time and energy in reassuring him and confirming his choices as being suitable. It seemed a very odd relationship.

This morning, it appeared he had a hangover. Complaining of a blinding headache, he spent much of the journey to the farm hidden from sight behind the morning's newspapers, which Rachel thought was hardly likely to aid his recovery.

Not far from Scaynes Hill, they turned down a narrow winding track for almost two miles before swinging through large ornamental gates of wrought ironwork. In fact, Rachel was to discover later that the family had derived their wealth from the sixteenth-century iron foundries, which swallowed so much of the ancient forest land of the Sussex Weald.

A wry smile flitted over her face as she recalled the image she'd had of the farm. Certainly nothing like this! Latimer Farm was a handsome building in warmly muted golden sandstone, with stone mullions and leaded lights in the windows. Huge slabs of Horsham stone tiled the roof and centuries of this enormous weight had bowed the oak timbers so that the roof undulated quaintly.

The car sighed to a halt on the half-moon driveway. To Rachel's right were pleasant formal gardens, with clipped yew hedges and lavender bushes dividing rose-beds and grass walks.

'You'd better come in and meet everyone,' growled Iván.

The large hall was warm and cosy, with a huge log fire blazing in the massive stone fireplace, throwing dancing lights on to the highly polished parquet floor.

'Well, dang me,' said a pleasant voice to her right. 'The dreaded Colombian knife-act has found a decent woman at last.'

'Very funny,' snapped Iván.

Rachel smiled politely at the young tousle-haired and untidy blond man, whose grey eyes didn't strip her naked as Iván's often did, but lit up in gentle admiration.

'My brother, Tony Latimer.'

'I am *not* your brother!' cried Tony. 'I won't admit to any blood tie with you!'

'Admit it or not,' said Iván unperturbed, 'it exists. Tony, this is Mrs Wells, my chauffeur.' His tone had become menacing.

Confused, Rachel shook Tony's hand. What was going on here?

'Chauffeur, eh?' grinned Tony. 'Feel free to drive me crazy any time.'

'You'll keep your eyes and hands off her,' snapped Iván.

Rachel quailed at the leashed anger in his body that threatened to explode into a terrible fury at any moment. The two brothers were acting like circling dogs. It was extraordinary.

'I'll do what I damn well please,' defied Tony.

'Not with Mrs Wells, you won't!' His glance swept sneeringly over Tony's shirt, that had come untucked from his trousers, watching with a derisive eye as it was stuffed back into the waistband. He spoke very softly, forcing the slender Tony to poke his head forwards and strain to hear. He loved to dominate people and put them at a disadvantage, thought Rachel with scorn. 'She works for me. Leave her alone or there'll be trouble.'

Tony's eyebrows lifted in mock astonishment. 'You have a personal interest?'

'No!' breathed Iván. His head was thrown back a little, the firelight playing on his high South American cheekbones and blue-black hair. There was a primitive flare to his nostrils and he stood with his hands on his hips, pushing back the dark navy vented jacket. Rachel sensed danger. He was exceptionally angry; she'd not seen that sensually cruel curve of his mouth before, nor the warning gleam in his eyes.

'Surely you, of all people, aren't objecting to the possibility that a Latimer might want to take out an employee?' said Tony with meaning.

Iván's breath hissed in dramatically. Tony drew back warily, as if he was dicing with death. Why was Iván so incredibly angry?

'Oh, God! You two aren't arguing already?' A tall, fiftyish blonde, squeak-smart and frowning, had emerged from another room off the hall. 'Darling Iván,' she sighed, accepting his triple kiss, 'I love to see you, but the atmosphere does tend to become heated wherever you are.'

'Tony enjoys provoking me, as you well know,' he glowered.

'Mother,' broke in Tony, 'meet Mrs Wells. This is Diana Latimer, my mother.'

So Tony's mother wasn't siding with him, in his hatred of Iván! Diana's genuine delight at seeing a man who was hated by her son was odd, to say the least. Rachel shook Diana's hand thoughtfully, wondering how Iván had talked his stepmother around. No doubt he'd used that amazing charm he reserved for special occasions; when he turned it on, no one could resist him. Despite Diana's cool reserve, Rachel thought she looked honest and straightforward, and they exchanged cautiously friendly smiles while Rachel frantically tried to work out the family relationships. Diana had obviously married Iván's father, and Tony and Emily were their children. But Tony had claimed that Iván wasn't his half-brother! It was all very strange.

'We weren't expecting you this weekend,' said Diana hesitantly. 'Not with Emily extending the holiday yet again.'

Iván grew white and still.

'Oh, dear,' said Diana agitatedly. 'You did know, I asked Tony to...' Her hand went to her mouth as Iván rounded furiously on Tony.

'You *bastard*!' said Iván with an evil growl. 'You and Emily do know how to turn the screws, don't you? You know damn well I can't come down next weekend because of the charity show.'

'Sorry,' said Tony casually. 'I forgot.'

'Like hell you did, you vindictive swine!' breathed
Iván.

Rachel was shocked at the venom in his voice. 'Perhaps
someone would show me my room,' she said miserably.
She hated rows. Iván and Tony seemed to be at daggers
drawn, and she wanted nothing to do with either of them.

'I will,' said Iván tightly.

'Mind your own business. I'm the host,' snapped
Tony. 'While you're here, you'll remember that this is
my house and you're a guest, Iván Posada! I inherited
Latimer's. I own it.'

The room chilled with the deadly hush that followed
his words. Diana was plucking nervously at her belt, and
Iván's coal-black eyes stood out in a white, strained face.
Rachel caught her breath at his expression of pure malice.

'Sure, you own it,' he said, in a whisper that shivered
with the violence that lay just beneath the surface, 'but
don't ever forget that our father wanted Latimer's to be
mine. Mine, because he loved my mother! I have a moral
right to be in this house, and you only have a legal one.
You remember *that* next time you try to throw me out!'

CHAPTER THREE

It was Diana who took Rachel to the coach-house, and apologised for the scene with a preoccupied air. She was obviously anxious to return to the house in case the brothers came to blows. Rachel had always found it extraordinary how families rowed so much. They were lucky to have each other. She'd always wanted to be part of a real family. This one seemed fraught with resentment and backbiting—and some unexplained puzzles. It was awful how Tony had rubbed in Iván's lost inheritance, which was presumably due to the fact that Iván wasn't a legitimate child. But then it wouldn't surprise her in the least to know that Tony had been the recipient of some pretty scathing attacks in the past. It was difficult for an outsider to know who'd started the whole sordid business.

She frowned as she unpacked her overnight bag. If Iván's father had wanted *him* to have Latimer's when he died, why on earth hadn't he said so in his will? He could leave the place to whoever he liked. Her hands stilled in the act of folding a sweater. Iván could have been lying, or maybe it was obvious that Iván wouldn't look after Diana, or the rest of the family. Maybe...

Rachel smiled wryly. Speculation was pointless. Instead, she'd enjoy the weekend in the country. She looked around in satisfaction.

The coach-house was a simple building, set in a cobbled yard, its whitewashed limestone walls covered in ivy. The interior had been kept as near to the original style as possible, and the natural brick floors looked well

47

in the galleried living-room, where the old carriages had once been kept. After unpacking, Rachel made a cup of tea and tried to avoid analysing the family set-up. Still, she'd need to understand the undercurrents of jealousy and sibling rivalry if she was to chauffeur them all around, so she'd talk to one of the staff when she got the chance. The inheritance was obviously a bone of contention and an old wound.

Yet her own reaction had astonished her more than anything. When Tony was being threatened by his brother, she should have felt scorn for Iván's vindictiveness. Instead, she'd been irrationally on his side, despite the fact that he was patently in the wrong. She sighed. Perhaps the strong feeling of loyalty she'd developed for her boss was overriding common sense.

There was a knock on the half-door and a blond head appeared. 'Mrs Wells? Everything OK?'

'Mr Latimer! Yes, come in, please.'

'Tony—I want you to call me Tony.'

'Well...'

'Please,' he coaxed. 'You're Rachel, I believe? Formalities are all right for arrogant bastards like Iván, but not me.'

'I—it's common practice in London, for...'

'I know, I know. It's still stupid in this day and age,' he said, brushing aside her rather heated explanation. 'Is that tea? I'd love some.'

'Oh. Yes.' She frowned at her defence of Iván.

'He doesn't change, does he? I don't know how you work for the bastard,' said Tony, sitting at the scrubbed beech table and watching her as she found her way around the china cupboard.

'I enjoy my work,' she said quickly. 'He has an awful headache today.'

'Excuses? Very loyal. He usually gets a headache when he comes down here. He hates to see me installed as the owner. Are you frowning because I'm slanging your boss, or because you don't know what the hell I'm talking about?'

'Both, really,' she said honestly.

Tony laughed. 'I suppose you've read about his shady current life in the newspapers, but few people know of his shady past. I'll tell you, and then you'll know why he's so sour.'

'I don't understand why he's the older brother and you inherited the property,' she said.

'He's *not* my brother!' bit Tony angrily. 'He's not related at all!'

'But . . .'

'Listen to the family history. My grandparents took on a Colombian maid called Teresa. She was a promiscuous little tart and my father fell for her sexy ways. She was sacked because of the way she was corrupting him. Later she turned up with her kid—Iván—claiming it was Father's. By then, my father had married my mother, Diana.'

'Why are you so sure he isn't your half-brother?'

'My grandparents knew Teresa had been sleeping around with half the staff, let alone what she got up to when she left. She was just trying to grab some maintenance. No chance of that! She kept bringing him around, never giving up hope. He was a savage child— nothing like Father at all. I remember Iván's rages of sensational fury. Be careful, Rachel, he's lethal stuff: unorthodox, uncontainable and one hell of an enemy. I know, I have the scars.'

Pity welled up inside her. Iván had said that his father didn't want him. What kind of upbringing must he have experienced, as the illegitimate son of a woman like

Teresa, with no means of support? No wonder he was bitter. And yet he was wealthy now. Somehow Rachel knew that his wealth had been hard won, by sheer ruthless determination to carve a path through life and bend it to his iron will. He frightened her more than ever, and she admired him more than ever, too.

'Is his mother still alive?' she asked.

'Yes, as bitter as ever, but not in this country, thank God. Teresa went back to Bogotá after my father died. Don't feel sorry for either of them, Rachel. They've hounded our family unmercifully. Iván went berserk at my father's funeral for no reason at all, and it took two hefty estate workers to calm him down.'

Rachel was silent. It all sounded reasonable, the way Tony was saying it, but something was wrong somewhere. Yet... Iván was a difficult man, and Tony was obviously very open and easy-going. It was impossible to believe that the story wasn't true. So why was there a nasty taste in her mouth?

'You apparently haven't seen Iván explode, and I hope you never do. It's like being in the path of a tornado. He unleashes his scouring envy and bitterness on everything within reach. This has been difficult,' said Tony, taking her hand. 'You see, I'm not vindictive, like Iván. But you need to be warned about him.'

The door was suddenly flung open and a furious Iván stood in the opening.

'I thought I'd find you here, Tony,' he said softly. 'Get your things, Mrs Wells, we're returning to London. There's no reason for us to stay.'

He looked pointedly at Tony's hand, holding Rachel's, and she gave a nervous tug, but Tony tightened his grip. 'You're being childish...' he began.

'I employ Mrs Wells. Let go of her and keep out of this,' Iván grated, and turned his fierce eyes on her.

With some irritation at the way Tony hung on to her to annoy his half-brother, she snatched her hand free and silently collected her things, then carried her cup to the sink.

'I'll do that,' said Tony quietly. 'I'll clear up. You'd better go before you're thrashed for disobedience.'

She flicked a quick look at Iván's set face. 'Thank you,' she said.

'See you next weekend, when Anna returns—oh, you can't make it, can you?' said Tony blandly.

Rachel had been shocked at the anguish in Iván's eyes, and then wondered if she'd been imagining it, since the hooded lids dropped before lifting again to reveal his habitual cynicism.

'Careful, Tony,' he breathed, making Tony lean forwards to listen. 'You don't want to end up on your back with your face rearranged.' He fingered the scar on his high cheekbone. 'I have one or two debts unpaid as yet.'

'I'm ready,' said Rachel brightly. 'Goodbye, Tony.' She moved towards the door. Iván's mouth twisted mockingly and then he turned on his heel, while Rachel breathed a sigh of relief.

Surprisingly, the week ran smoothly. To begin with, she didn't see Iván apart from brief mealtimes, because he shut himself in his study and worked solidly. Rachel knew now why he was so vitriolic in print: he was working out his envy and disappointment. It was hard to be disowned by your parents—she knew, neither of hers had claimed *her*. Although she understood his hollow emptiness, and realised that he must have learnt bitterness at his mother's breast, his behaviour did lessen him in her eyes, and she was strangely miserable that the man she had begun to build up into someone to admire had feet of clay, after all.

But after a couple of days he made up for his bad behaviour at the farm by being rather charming and easy to get on with for the rest of the week. This was almost worse, because their eyes kept meeting again amid long, tense, significant silences. He'd ask her opinion often and listen in flattering seriousness to her earnest replies. It was as though he valued and trusted her. Several times she risked making a rather old-fashioned and sincere observation, half hoping that he'd laugh scornfully and take with his laugh her rising sensation of mental intimacy. But he didn't. He responded with unnervingly sensitive insight that led her to believe he really might be soft and vulnerable beneath that confident and cynical veneer he showed to the world.

When he told her of his plans for the weekend, and that they didn't include her in any way, she was horrified at her sense of disappointment.

'I shan't need you from four o'clock on Friday till Monday morning,' he said. 'I'm being collected by a limousine for the UNICEF jamboree. Every year I write a comedy play for their charity night. That's on Friday. Then, on Saturday I'll be in Hatchard's, churning out cartoons which'll be auctioned. Sunday, I help to entertain some of the UNICEF workers as a "thank you" by the Committee. You're welcome to use the car as much as you like—go off on a trip, if you want.'

'Can't I come to see any of this?' she asked.

His eyes rested on her, his expression impassive. 'No. If you're still with me next year, I'll get you tickets. This year it's too late—we're booked up solid. We should make a lot of money. Would you really have been interested?'

Rachel thought there was a touch of wistfulness in his final, casually thrown away sentence, as though he hoped she was, and it made her uncharacteristically impulsive.

'Very much. I hope I'm with you next year. I'd love to see the play and everything else. It sounds wonderful.'

She reeled from the dazzling smile that lit his dark face. A painful stab of attraction whistled through her body. When he was happy, Iván was perfectly irresistible. And very dangerous to her equilibrium.

On Friday evening she felt unaccountably lonely when he left; he looked devastatingly handsome in a dark pinstripe suit. She caught herself wishing she was with him, and tried to push him out of her mind. It was like missing a difficult and untrained dog, she told herself. He took up so much of her mental energy that she was bound to miss him. She switched on the TV news and found that they were featuring the UNICEF charity weekend. Iván was mentioned with awe and affection, many of the organisers referring to him and saying how hard and untiringly he'd worked over the years for the disadvantaged children of the world.

Rachel listened avidly, learning a little more about her volatile employer. It was, perhaps, because of his own troubled background that he'd devoted so much of his precious and valuable time in this way. Whatever the reason, he'd earned hard cash for UNICEF and made a lot of children laugh and forget their troubles for a while. She found herself smiling happily, when the phone rang.

'Hi, Rachel, it's Tony.'

'Oh! Hello!' How odd that she should be disappointed. Secretly she knew she'd been hoping that it was Iván, and that he needed her.

'I've just discovered that Iván's away. Made any plans?'

'No,' said Rachel, depressed. 'I thought I'd wash my hair and that kind of thing.'

'Good lord! Why not come down here? You can meet the family informally, and get to know Anna. You'll need to, if you're to drive her around. It's a fantastic opportunity to do so without Iván around, because he always monopolises her time. She might find it frightening, being driven by a stranger. Besides, Diana and I would like to see you. Come as a kind of guest.'

'I—I don't think...'

'Shall I order you?' It sounded as though Tony was grinning. 'With Iván away, I'm your boss now. Please. It makes sense.'

'Yes, it does,' she admitted. It might cheer her up and show her that her sense of loss was more to do with loneliness than anything else. So she agreed, and left a note for Iván, who'd said he wasn't sure what time he'd be back on the Sunday.

Emily had Tony's thin, blonde untidiness. Mike, her husband, was short, stocky and rather serious. He was very wrapped up in the farm. Emily was a good hostess and welcomed Rachel warmly. Little Anna had her father's dark, blue-black straight hair and, like him, didn't automatically set out to charm strangers. She seemed very sullen. Emily kept apologising to Anna for the fact that Iván wasn't there to greet them on return from their holiday, but Anna's face grew steadily angrier and angrier. Rachel began to explain that Iván was working to help poor children, but Emily suddenly broke in and claimed it was Anna's bedtime.

Rachel offered to help put her to bed, hoping to make some kind of bond, but Emily wouldn't hear of it. Tony had insisted that Rachel ate dinner with them, and it was then that she learned Iván's wife had died. One day, when she knew them all a little better, she'd ask why Emily was looking after Iván's child.

The weekend went well. Tony was very pleasant and, although it had taken a lot of work, he finally got Emily to agree that he and Rachel could take Anna out. Privately, Rachel thought that Emily was a little over-protective of the little girl, and a bit possessive, but she kept that to herself.

She helped Anna to make waxed paper boats and sail them on the lake at the bottom of the valley, getting very muddy in the process. Tony flirted outrageously and made her laugh, and in the evening they played Scrabble together in the coach-house. It was all very pleasant and the countryside was balm to Rachel's highly tuned emotions.

Sunday was spent almost exclusively in Tony's company, and he showed her around the farm. It was after a lunch of scrambled eggs on toast at the coach-house, that Tony got a little too fresh. Standing at the sink, her hands in the washing-up water, she had been unable to stop him from putting down the tea-towel and placing his hands on her waist.

'Don't, please,' she said quickly, Iván's words coming to mind.

'Can't help it,' he said sadly. 'You're awfully tempting.' He dropped a kiss on her neck and she flinched, shaking the suds from her fingers in an attempt to stave him off. 'I don't want to frighten you off, Rachel,' he said in a low tone, 'only let you know I think you're fantastic. A girl in a million.'

She was astonished. 'Tony!'

'I know,' he grinned, releasing her and moving away, leaning on the draining-board. 'A bit too soon for that kind of statement. OK. Now you know and we can forget it. Do you like the farm?'

Rachel's eyes warmed. 'Very much. It's lovely. When I was a child, I dreamed of living on a farm. I love the countryside. It doesn't seem to matter if you're alone when you go for walks, there's something friendly about it, not like wandering around London—even the parks.'

'I'm glad you like it,' said Tony. 'I hope you'll spend a lot of time here.'

There was an awkward pause, because his words seemed to carry more meaning than she could fathom out, but she was saved from commenting by the phone.

'I need you back here.' Iván's crackling fury reached her, even down the line.

Rachel's hackles rose. Typical of him! No question of apologising for breaking into her weekend! He called, and expected her to run.

'Are you there? Did you hear?' snapped Iván.

'Yes, sir,' she said coolly. Tony raised his eyebrows and gave a wry grin. 'Straight away?' she added.

'Yes. You did say you'd work antisocial hours, so I'm not asking you to do anything you haven't already agreed to. I gather you're entertaining Tony,' he said in a grim voice. 'Put him on.'

Longing to shock him with her rich vocabulary of swear words, which she had learnt from various foster brothers and sisters, she relinquished the phone and stalked to her bedroom to get her things together. This, she thought, was a replay of the last time she'd been at the farm. If Iván was going to do this whenever she got friendly with Tony, she'd have to point out that he was being petty. It was a side of his character she didn't want to see. Being snobbish about people of different backgrounds mixing was horrid and unworthy.

From the faltering way Tony was speaking, it sounded as though Iván was giving his brother a tongue-lashing. Rachel grew tight-lipped. When she left, Tony was still listening, red-faced. He gave her a rueful goodbye. She smiled broadly, to show her sympathy, and he retaliated by blowing her a cheeky kiss in fun.

Iván's anger hadn't abated when she arrived. Before she'd even turned off the engine, he had barged through the entrance doors to the apartment block and flung himself into the back of the car.

'Drive,' he rapped.

'Where to, sir?' she asked sweetly.

'Anywhere. Just drive.'

Holding her tongue, she obeyed, hoping for his sake that there was a better reason for her to drive all the way up to London than spiting his brother, or to give him a car ride. If it had been anyone else, she would have driven to a quiet spot, perhaps near the river or one of the parks. For him, she chose the centre of London and did her best to get caught in traffic jams. The vibes coming from the back seat were definitely chilly.

'All right, Mrs Wells, very funny,' he said wearily. 'Take me to Hyde Park Corner and drop me at the top of Rotten Row. I'll walk down it. Pick me up at the other end.'

She sat in the car, watching him stride off with a long, feral swing. Even from this distance, the set of his body showed that he was still raging internally. Something had made him very, very mad. It didn't bode well for her at all.

Somehow, when she parked the car and strolled off to find him, she found her wariness and impatience with his irascibility changing to pity. It wasn't his fault that he didn't know how to be nice to people. No one had been particularly nice to him. She stopped abruptly. Iván was sitting on a bench, leaning forwards, in an attitude of dejection. A rush of sympathy softened her heart.

'Mr Posada?' she said timidly, standing close to the brooding man.

He looked up, startled, with pained eyes. 'Please sit down, Mrs Wells,' he said quietly.

He seemed to be struggling with himself, as if choosing words was difficult. Or perhaps he was uncertain whether to speak his mind or not. Uncertain? Iván Posada? Rachel's steady eyes rested speculatively on him.

Then the big shoulders rose and fell, and he sat back against the wooden slats, staring into the distance. 'There is something I must warn you about,' he said.

It seemed to be a brotherly trait, she thought, arranging herself carefully on the seat.

'I didn't want to say this,' he said hesitantly. 'I want you to be aware that... Hell!' He was silent, staring into space and chewing on his lip. 'My brother. You like him?'

'Well, yes, he seems very nice.'

Iván placed his hands on her shoulders and turned her to face him, their knees bumping. Rachel's heart began to hammer rapidly as she absorbed the full energising power of his intimidating body. She resisted his pull, trying to lean back, but his fingers bit into her shoulders and held her prisoner.

'He's not,' he said simply.

Rachel wondered how to deal with this. Her lashes dropped over her eyes, to conceal how disappointed she was. And how violently she was reacting to the closeness of his body.

'Look at me,' he ordered. *'Look!'*

She raised her eyes to see pain and fury there. And something else, something indefinable.

'I had no idea Tony would latch on to you so quickly,' he said in his soft voice. 'When I suggested you took a trip, I didn't expect it to be to Latimer Farm!'

'It seemed a good opportunity to get to know Anna,' said Rachel, jumping as he flinched. 'Tony thought...'

'Tony,' he said bitterly. 'All Tony wants is a wife. It doesn't matter particularly what she's like, as long as she's reasonably presentable.'

Sickened by his words, she had turned her head away, but his hand reached out and held her jaw in a vicelike grip, forcing her to meet his impassioned gaze.

'I know it's unbelievable. If you're not careful, you will be married to a man who doesn't love you. And that I will not tolerate,' he said in a dangerous tone. 'If he comes on strong, resist him. Understand?'

'Perfectly, sir,' she managed, fighting down the urge to slap his hand away. 'But you're imagining things.'

'The flirting? The hand-holding? I wish to God I hadn't taken on a woman,' he muttered under his breath.

Rachel's eyes closed momentarily in apprehension. 'Mr Posada,' she said, looking directly at him with all the sincerity she could muster, 'I'm not remotely interested in men. I've been hurt and don't intend to go through all that again. All I want to do is get on with the job. I am your chauffeur and that is as far as my contact will go with the rest of your family.'

Iván's hand had slackened as she spoke and now it stayed, curved around her chin, as he considered her words. 'You do like this job, don't you?' he stated softly.

'You know I do.'

'Hmm. As long as you don't go for higher stakes,' he said cryptically, releasing her.

Rachel jumped up at once. 'Where to now, sir?' she asked briskly, wishing the slide of his hand over her skin hadn't sent her pulses racing.

'Colombian Embassy, Hans Crescent,' he said as he strode lithely alongside her. 'I'm glad you're not interested in Tony. Very, very glad.'

His voice was soft and honey-warm. She remained silent, shocked at the way she trembled in response to his words.

'When I've been to the Embassy, we'll have to pop in on my office. I recalled you because I have been asked unexpectedly to do some radio interviews and two breakfast-time television appearances. We'll go through the schedule together.'

Later, seated in his untidy office, Rachel began to see how he needed to work in overdrive all the time. If he didn't, he'd never get through all his work. Iván had rummaged through the papers on his desk and pulled out some letters.

'Now,' he said, picking up a big chart and looking around for space. 'Here.' He came around to Rachel's side of the desk and knelt on the floor, opening out the paper and holding its edges down with books at each corner. It was a huge timetable. 'Have a look at this.'

A little nervously, Rachel knelt beside him. He had removed his jacket and she had been treated to the un-compromisingly male stretch of his shoulders as he bent over the schedule. It didn't seem too good an idea to get close to him, but there wasn't much alternative because the writing on the chart was so small.

'Ignore whatever's written in black. Those are the deadlines,' he said. 'Pay attention to the red entries. To-night.' He jabbed a long finger at the middle of the paper and Rachel began to make sense of the timetable, seeing where the days began and ended and how packed his schedule was for the next week. 'Interview with David Frost. Then the television studio at the crack of dawn and on to Broadcasting House.' He turned to his desk and slid down a notepad. 'Write down the times, the destinations and work out when we need to leave.'

'Yes, sir,' she replied, wondering why he had been singled out for such attention.

Heat was pouring out of his body, distracting her as she checked and double-checked the entries. She was conscious that his shoulder was a millimetre away from hers, his arm tautly supporting his weight as he knelt forwards, the big hand with its long, sensitive fingers spread out on the paper in front of her. She gave a shudder to think of that hand exploring her spine, lifting her shirt and curving around her breasts.

'Aren't you curious, Mrs Wells?'

She jumped, and looked at him, startled. His eyes were sultry, his expression smouldering and that damn tongue of his was hovering at the corner of his mouth again. 'What about?' she asked shakily.

'The interviews.'

Her relief was palpable. 'Yes, sir.'

He laughed and stood up, holding out his hand. She wished she hadn't taken it, because in helping her up he drew her slowly up his body—not quite touching it, but too close, nevertheless. 'This is why,' he said softly, pushing a book into her free hand.

Rachel took the opportunity to move away and direct her mind to the book he'd written, giving satirical pen sketches of heads of state throughout the world, accompanied by some deadly cartoons.

'You can keep that,' he said casually.

'Thank you, sir.' She was pleased with the book, but showed not one iota of emotion. She dared not. Give this man one millionth of an inch and he'd take a thousand miles.

'Don't bust a gut with excitement. They gave me twelve free copies,' he said laconically. 'Now get me home. I have to shower, change and get something to eat before this interview.'

Rachel was more nervous than he was. In fact, to look at Iván, you'd never know he was on his way to take part in a programme that was watched by millions of people. All through the transmission, she watched from the audience, chewing her lip. She needn't have worried. Iván's brand of humour went down well with David Frost, and his electric personality had created a tingling *frisson* throughout the studio. Rachel relaxed and began to enjoy his barbed comments.

'How do you think it went?' he asked the moment he saw her, when she came to collect him in the hospitality room.

'Very well, sir,' she said politely.

'You don't think I was over the top? Did you like the joke about the llama?'

Rachel grinned at the memory. 'Everyone roared,' she said.

'Yes, I know. Did you?'

She stopped, confused. Why the hell should he care? 'Yes, I did,' she said. 'You were very funny.'

'Hmm,' he said, his eyes gleaming. 'Not outrageous?'

'I'm sure the switchboard is jammed with people complaining,' she said.

'Good,' he smiled in satisfaction. 'Have a drink.'

'No, thank you.'

'Ver-r-ry good,' he mocked. 'Take me home.'

He called his goodbyes and followed her to the car. The other interviews followed a similar pattern. Iván was calm, Rachel was nervous; he amused everyone vastly and drew huge laughs from studio audiences. Rachel admired his sang-froid enormously—though if you were arrogant and didn't care what other people thought of you, she supposed it wasn't hard to remain at ease. Each time, she was quizzed about her favourite moments, and they laughed together at the memory. Hectic it was, but very, very rewarding. Unnervingly so. Rachel knew this man's faults, and they were many, but she was finding that his extraordinarily powerful dynamism swept those faults out of sight.

She was beginning to enjoy talking to him, sharing ideas and opinions over the breakfast table. The tension was holding them apart and drawing them together at the same time. If she read or heard of anything amusing, she found herself storing it up deliberately in her memory, to tell him later. He'd thrust newspaper articles in front of her, angrily pointing out an injustice, and watch her response. It was all very disconcerting. They were becoming too close, and her growing reliance on Iván to illuminate her life was frightening. She'd have to cool down the relationship. But how did you cool down a simmering volcano with a fathomless well of boiling magma ready to overwhelm the unwary?

Then came the night of the reception at the Colombian Embassy. Rachel's calm was rattled early on in the evening. Iván had walked into the kitchen where she was waiting, dressed in an immaculate dinner-jacket and looking blackly satanic. Her teeth bit into her soft lower lip when she saw the black bow-tie in his hands, and the look of pleasant enquiry on his face.

'I wonder, Mrs Wells, if you . . .' He held out the tie, one eyebrow raised hopefully.

'I'm sorry, I can't do those things,' she said abruptly. She was darned if he'd tantalise her like that! He was the kind of man who could fix bow-ties blindfold.

'If I bend down a little . . .' His hands were on her shoulders, splaying out and heating her delicate bones, his velvet eyes glowing warmly and that sensual mouth curving deliciously. 'Please.'

She'd try—and make a mess of it, she thought savagely, then he wouldn't ask her again.

'What great big eyes you've got,' he murmured.

Rachel made sure her great big eyes glittered angrily.

'You'd be quite good-looking if you . . .'

He stopped, alerted by her narrow glance, and gagged as she jerked the tie very tight. His hand clamped over hers and squeezed till she gasped and shot him a pleading look.

'Try again,' he said huskily. 'Get it right this time.'

It was a warning, and she knew it. Seething at being his valet as well as his chauffeur, she reached both hands up, knowing how her breasts were straining against the fine fabric of the blouse and that her body was as near as it could be without actually touching him. The service was an intimate and unwelcome one. As quickly as she could, she folded over the black cloth, ignoring but not immune to the carved jaw, the gently breathing mouth and his steadying hands that had now begun to slide down her arms.

Rachel's hands began to fumble and she drew her brows together in frustration.

'Something wrong?' he mocked.

'Nothing,' she grated. 'There.' Quickly she moved back and slipped into her jacket with a haste that amused him vastly.

It was worse later. He'd been drinking a good deal that evening. Whether it was relief because he'd finished all his promotional appearances, or he'd missed the company of women during the hectic week, she wasn't sure, but when he insisted on sitting in the passenger seat on the way home, she was uncomfortably aware that there was a different, dangerous quality about him, as if he intended to break a few rules. The Bentley drew away smoothly and Rachel concentrated intently on the road.

'What a perfect servant you are,' he taunted, black eyes dancing.

Rachel noted the husky voice and took warning. 'Thank you, sir,' she said politely.

He smiled mockingly. 'Does nothing get you mad?'

'Not much, sir. Nothing you would know about.'

'Stop here.'

Fear gathered in Rachel's stomach. It was the early hours of the morning and the street was quite deserted. She pulled over to the kerb and cut the engine.

'We'll have a talk. Look at me.'

Warily, Rachel faced him, the fear reaching her eyes.

'Tony's been bleating on about Anna's school rota. I'm going to let you drive down there tomorrow... today,' he amended, looking at his watch. 'But...' He spotted something on Rachel's blouse—she'd been eating pastries in the embassy kitchen—and reached out a hand to see what it was. 'My apologies,' he murmured, his fingers remaining on the material. 'I seem to have rubbed the grease in.'

She was unable to move. A hidden thread drew them together, forcing her to focus on his deep soulful eyes, knowing how his carved mouth had parted in sensual desire. Take your fingers away, she thought, closing her eyes. Their tips are burning through to my skin.

'It's all right,' she said weakly.

'No, it's not,' he breathed. 'It's not all right at all.'

And then his fingers were sliding up the silken skin of her jaw, to her ear, and she could smell the alcohol on his breath as it lightly fanned her face.

He mustn't kiss her, she must prevent him. If he did, she'd be obliged to leave and go through that awful business of job hunting again. She cowered back against the door. 'Don't, I beg you...'

'Delicious. I like it when a woman begs.' He slipped his hand behind her head, cradling it, and Rachel could feel the imprint of every finger.

'I don't want to lose my job,' she said shakily.

'Then let me kiss you,' he said reasonably.

'You arrogant...!'

'Better. Less perfect,' he said throatily.

His index finger had pressed against her mouth, and Rachel did her utmost not to groan at the urge to take it into her mouth and deal with it as she wanted to, tasting it, biting it, sucking... Damn his hide! Only a swine would take advantage of an employee like this.

'Nothing personal, Mrs Wells,' he said lazily. 'I'm doing you a good turn. You see, if I'm letting you loose in Tony's company, you need something for comparison. I don't trust him.'

His ruthless hands yanked her body against his at the same time that pressure on the back of her head ground her mouth into his in a fierce possession, imprinting itself for ever. Without gentleness, he forced open her mouth, his tongue hungering within her soft sweetness, ferocious in its intent. Rachel kept her body stiff and unyielding, making herself ice out the wild flurries of desire that shafted to her womb. His onslaught increased, his kisses deepened, and Rachel's head began to whirl as his touch gentled, became more persuasive and far more dangerous.

Despite herself, even though she knew it was madness, her treacherous body responded visibly, stirring, writhing a little, and Iván's mouth softened against hers, coaxing and teasing.

This was what she'd wanted for a long time, she realised dazedly. Now it was really happening, she could recognise her hungry longing for what it was. His tongue swept seductively into her mouth, spicy-sweet and probing.

He stifled a groan and gave in to the sheer pleasure of her tender lips, devouring hotly the slender neck, sliding his tongue between her neat white collar and her feverish skin.

Small moans were tearing from her throat, despite her frantic search for control. He was using her to slake his lust. In his half-inebriated state he'd forgotten who she was. Her protesting hands fluttered against his chest and he sat back, his eyes pure obsidian.

'Now the question is,' he said in a smoky voice, 'was that response for me, or because you're ripe for anyone to pluck?'

Speechless with rage, Rachel immediately snapped out of her dreamy state and switched on the ignition with trembling, cold fingers. But Iván's hand was holding the gear lever and she couldn't escape him that easily. For a wonderful, unbelievable moment, she'd thought he was really attracted to her. In the softening of his body, the tender way he had begun to kiss her, she'd been crazy enough to believe he'd been acting impulsively, and the feelings that had filled her brain and body had been sensational. Huh! Iván was about as impulsive as Machiavelli.

'I think you ought to stop this,' she said, with remarkable control over her voice. Inside her, a small explosion was occurring! 'You're drunk and you're insulting me.'

'We'll go when you answer my question,' he persisted.

'What question?' she asked coldly.

'Who was that response for? Any man, because you're hungry? Or me?' The last two words growled out of his throat, with raw desire, rocking Rachel with their feeling.

'You...you must know that you are a very skilful man and can probably knock most women off balance momentarily,' she said shakily. 'I neither want sex, nor want you. I can't work for you any longer, Mr Posada, since you subject me to such humiliation.'

'Many women would be thrilled,' he mocked.

'I am not many women.'

'No. And, since I'm a little drunk, you must forgive this assault on your virtue. It never happened. Unless Tony kisses you. Then you will remember it.'

She flicked a withering glare at him and deliberately wiped her hand across her mouth, as if to erase all trace of his marauding lips. 'It's not something I would wish to remember.'

'No?' Iván's eyes were calculating. 'You will. I'll make damn sure of that.'

CHAPTER FOUR

GENERALLY, Rachel's time with five-year-old Anna was limited to the short journeys to school, when she picked up a number of other children en route. She noticed that Anna chatted normally then; it was only with the adults at the farm that she was ultra-reticent. Rachel was conscious of the way the dark-eyed child stared implacably, so like her father that it made shivers run down her back. Yet there was the same dynamic charisma, too, that drew her to Anna, and they'd spend all too brief periods together, letting their hair down, fooling around by the lake. Then, when Rachel had helped Anna to clean herself up in order to meet Emily's exacting standards of tidiness, the shutters would come down over Anna's eyes, and she was remote and uncommunicative again.

With Tony, she was always on her guard, as though Iván's vindictive warning might be based on fact. When Diana returned to her flat in Brighton, Tony's attentions intensified. Several times he made a pass at her, or flattered her too intimately. When he did, she was haunted by the image of a dark, brooding man. Iván.

She missed him, and that was ludicrous. Rachel worried over the way she longed to see him again when they were apart, and how she was alternately irritated and fascinated by him when they were together. She must widen her horizons a bit, even clear the air with Tony so that he knew she wasn't interested in him sexually, but as a friend. That would lift the sensation she had with Iván that the walls were closing in on them both and driving them together. That would prevent her mouth from drying when he came near, and stop her heart lifting with joy when she saw him.

Iván was too dangerous a man to desire. Rachel's self-confidence wasn't strong enough to withstand rejection again—and rejection she would get. For, if she did pick up his sensual and subtle invitations, she had no doubt that such an intelligent and witty man would only play with her briefly for her curiosity value. She might as well get used to that idea and turn her mind outwards, instead of inwards, and stop imbuing their relationship with romantic fantasies.

So, although she was fighting down the beginnings of a cold, she accompanied Tony into the countryside for a walk, intending to talk to him about his unwelcome flirting. Unfortunately she was feeling fragile, having skipped lunch, and her stomach seemed to be at sixes and sevens that morning, so it was all she could do to make normal conversation, let alone broach a difficult subject. Maybe it was the prospect of facing Iván again that daunted her; she certainly felt butterflies inside when she thought of seeing him again.

Tony helped her to pick some blackberries and an armful of scarlet hawthorn berries which she planned to arrange in the big Spode jug on the deep windowsill of the coach-house. After a couple of hours, a chilly mist drifted down and they decided to return. On the way back, he stopped on the edge of the beech copse and turned to her.

'Rachel,' he said slowly, 'you've been a bit offhand today. Has Iván said anything to make you wary of me?'

'I—I——' She chewed the inside of her lip, unable to lie.

'Damn him! You mustn't believe anything he says, you know. He's incorrigible. Any man who'd run out on his pregnant wife is a prize bastard.'

Rachel's eyes widened in shock. It couldn't be true! Tony's face and tone gave her the awful answer. He was sincere. No wonder Tony despised him; and now she did. 'You shouldn't be telling me this,' she muttered, turning to go, but Tony stayed her.

'Why? Because it hurts you? Because you care for him?'

'Tony, of course not! You must be insane to think that I could be interested in him as a man!'

At that moment, hurt and smarting, with Tony's damning words ringing in her ears, she meant that with all her heart and soul. A man who could abandon his wife, pregnant with his child, was beneath contempt. She loathed the way Iván had bemused her senses with his dark eyes and wildly exciting personality. He'd betrayed her trusting heart! She was angry that she'd been stupid enough to feel admiration and to imagine a growing closeness. How easy it was to delude yourself, she thought bitterly, if you wanted to be fooled.

'Thank God!' breathed Tony. 'I was afraid...'

'Please credit me with a little sense,' she said quietly.

He smiled, and with a quick movement trapped her against a tree, the weight of his body lying against her and his mouth gently murmuring against hers.

'Don't!' She wrenched her head away. 'I'll get the sack if Iván hears of this!'

'But he won't,' grinned Tony. 'How could he? X-ray eyes he might have, but he can't beam his lasers all the way down here from London. You know, Rachel, you're beginning to mean rather a lot to me. Between the two of us, I think I could be falling in love with you.'

'Tony, stop fooling around. You have to stop flirting with me.'

'I'm not. I'm serious.'

'You can't be! Oh, darn, I'm going to be late to pick up Iván. We really must get back or I won't get to London on time.' She passed a shaky hand over her forehead. Her body seemed to be burning up, and she didn't have the energy to argue with him. Maybe next time.

'You're trembling,' said Tony with satisfaction. 'Don't be afraid. I'm harmless.'

His lips brushed hers again and Rachel had no willpower to spurn him. Her head was a little giddy and there was a strange lethargy in her limbs. His kiss deepened and he sighed in pleasure.

'Wonderful,' he said gently. 'I've never known anyone like you before, Rachel. I do love you.'

'Please don't say that!'

In answer, he smiled and kissed her. But it was nothing like Iván's heart-stopping kiss. It didn't make her want to shock him with an abandoned response, it didn't make her burn like a torch, nor had every nerve begun to vibrate like the strings of a harp. And that worried her.

Despite her agitation, and the fact that he knew she was late, Tony asked her to drive to a chemist in Haywards Heath because he was out of aspirin. Rachel got some medication for herself while she was there. Her cold had bypassed her nose and sunk into her lungs. She felt very clammy and shaky.

By the time she handed over the aspirin and allowed Tony to squeeze her hand in warm affection as he said goodbye, she felt feverish. The damp air had chilled her to the bone, seeping into her vulnerable body. Mist swirled across the motorway, demanding her concentration on the road and forcing her speed down. In fact, she was so concerned with being late that she only noticed just in time that she was low on petrol. There was a long queue for the pumps and her fingers beat a jerky tattoo on the steering wheel as she waited for one to be free. She turned on the heater, feeling the warmth permeate her skin, then had to jump out soon after to unlock the petrol cap and get cold waiting to pay the attendant.

Iván was pacing up and down the foyer like a ravenous animal waiting for his prey, shooting a black, glittering look at her through the big glass doors as she crossed the pavement. Wishing she'd had something to eat, she lurched a little unsteadily past Daniel, who caught her waist and held her securely.

'Say, you look rough,' he said. 'Something wrong?'

Iván's lips compressed. 'Leave her alone!'

'I'm all right, just a little cold,' she said, as Daniel led her over to him, supporting her protectively.

Iván took the car keys from her cold fingers and thrust them at Daniel.

'Put the car in the garage, please. I don't think we'll be using it.'

'The door, sir... I'm responsible...'

Iván's eyes blazed briefly and Daniel disappeared posthaste. Rachel smiled weakly at Iván's logic. Desertion of one's job was all right as long as it was in Iván Posada's service!

'Sorry. I was held up in Haywards Heath,' she said.

'What the devil were you doing there?' he snapped.

'Tony needed some aspirin,' she said weakly.

'He never takes the stuff.'

'But...'

'A ruse, Mrs Wells, to make you late and annoy me. You'll get used to his little ways. Did he delay you with anything else?'

Her brain fumbled through clouds of cotton wool to understand.

'You look ravished. Or at least, you look as if I'd ravished you. Tony would never get that kind of result.'

An extraordinary weakness filled her body. These two men were playing games with her, batting her backwards and forwards between them in an attempt to score points. It was too silly. And what was that about ravishing? She took a wheezing breath and a wave of shivering hit her.

Iván's fearsome hand lay briefly on her forehead, and her heart pounded unnaturally in her ears.

'Please,' she mumbled, 'I . . . oh!'

She had staggered on buckling legs and been caught expertly by Iván, who swept her up in his arms as if she was a young child. At the door to the apartment, he struggled a little with the double locks which he had secured for the weekend, before he was finally able to kick the door open.

Helpless in his arms, as he strode angrily to her bedroom, Rachel felt terribly light-headed. Everything was happening in slow motion. Iván's smooth jaw hovered in pure carved bronze just near her mouth, his damaged cheekbone and eagle's nose carving dark lines above her fluttering lashes. The inside of her skull whirled around a few times and then her head became far too heavy to be held upright. It rolled into the warm column of his neck, her mouth sagging open and tasting the satin-smooth skin. How nice he felt. Her lips surreptitiously moved over his throat again, not trusting her judgement the first time. Still nice, she thought woozily. How could anyone feel so gorgeous on the outside, deliciously silky and sexy, and be so corrupt inside?

Her face breathed in his male smell, and her nose nuzzled for a more comfortable place; his ribcage rose alarmingly against her body, and the grip around her knees and arm tightened dramatically. Lovely warmth flooded into her blood, turning her flesh to the same consistency, and then her bones, till they all flowed in

one molten river in his arms. There was no division between their bodies at all; she felt none of the small in-
dications that ought to be telling her his grip was hurting
her, or that his breath was whispering on her face. There
was only the sensation of floating effortlessly together.

'Rachel...'

Was that him, she wondered, sounding so hoarse? Oh,
lord, what was she doing, spinning crazy dreams in her
head?

'Sorry... sir,' she muttered. 'Feel... funny.'

She was flung abruptly on to the bed and her heavy
eyes shot open with the shock. Iván towered over her,
glaring. Now she'd done it! Chauffeurs were useless if
they didn't chauff. Or whatever. The breath caught in
her throat, impeded by the hard lump there; Iván was
easing his tie and undoing his top button, exposing his
vulnerable, tanned throat and what must be warm skin,
just above his big, virile chest. Terror gripped her and
she forced hugely frightened eyes to follow his every
move till she could see him no longer. Oh, God! She
was helpless: ill, vulnerable, far too weak and woolly-
headed to fight him off. Why did he have to choose this
moment to take advantage of her? It was typical. She
must...

'Oh!'

'I didn't mean to startle you. Drink this.'

A brandy was held to her lips.

'No, I won't!' she mumbled thickly. Her tongue wasn't
obeying her brain.

Rachel tried to struggle up, and Iván's body bent
menacingly over her, as he leaned forwards and raised
her against the pillows.

'Do as you're told.' He pressed the rim of the glass
against her lips and glared.

Weakly, Rachel capitulated. It might help to give her strength. The brandy dropped immediately to her stomach, balling in brain-mashing heat, filling her limbs with a wonderful lethargy and her mind with silliness. She should have eaten.

'Feel better?' he glowered.

'No. Yes. Well... No!' And she never would if he continued to hover like that. Her hands went out and touched his shoulders, warm under the cotton shirt, fingers trailing over the tautened muscles. Her whole being seemed in a kind of boneless suspension. Rachel moaned, half-delirious, drugged by the fever, the drink, and the pulsating heat that flushed her face and kindled her eyes to a tawny flame. Someone was breathing harshly, and it turned out to be her. She forced ragged gasps through parched lips, the breath seething and spasmodic.

'God!' The word was wrung from Iván like a softly expelled breath. There was the suspicion of a touch on her hair, a moment's tenderness in his black eyes and then a veil drew over them. 'You're in one hell of a state,' he muttered.

Oh, I am, she thought. What is happening to me?

Then he abandoned her. His desertion tore away the interminable tension, leaving only an unbearable emptiness. Rachel tried to move her aching limbs, but she had lost all will-power. She shut her eyes, in the hope that sleep would bring relief.

Hard, hurting fingers woke her rudely, pressing a temperature strip to her forehead. She tried to prise the fingers off, but they refused to budge and continued the pressure.

'How long have you felt like this?' he said sharply.

I'm swimming, she thought. In his eyes. Two fingers grasped her chin.

'Ow! Like what?' she asked with a froglike croak.

'Dammit, you could have had an accident in these weather conditions,' he said furiously.

He was angry about the car. His precious status symbol. 'I drove as carefully as I could,' she said, concentrating on her words with as much of her woolly mind as she could summon up. Every muscle in her body screamed. Flu. Just her luck.

'Stupid woman,' was his unsympathetic remark. The mattress depressed as he sat down, and she rolled into his thigh. Such an intimate thing to do. 'Think you can get into bed?' he asked.

'Oh, dear,' she muttered. 'You were going home.'

'This is my home,' he snapped. 'I'll ring Tony.'

'No, please go. I'll stay here.'

'Don't be ridiculous. You can't look after yourself. You can hardly raise one arm. Get into bed while I telephone.'

Like a broken puppet, Rachel sat erect and immediately flopped back on to the pillows again. Iván was railing at Tony on the phone, his fury unconcealed. She blanched at the acidity of his tongue. Poor Tony! She put her hands over her ears and curled up to protect her throbbing head with the pillows. They were snatched rudely away.

'I distinctly remember ordering you to bed! Do you have a death wish? Flu I can cope with; you'll need to give me notice if you intend to develop pneumonia. Now *move*, Mrs Wells, while I make you a hot drink!'

'Tyrant,' she muttered sullenly, rolling languidly on to her tummy and managing—very slowly—to get on to all fours. Now what? Her sluggish brain refused to think.

'God save us!' breathed Iván, studying her position in evident pain.

She was pulled on to his lap, his thighs beautifully warm, his chest burning into her already fiery body. Impatient hands fiercely snapped buttons from holes and roughly hauled off her jacket. He bent to remove her shoes, his fingers sliding sensually down the sensitive skin of her legs and she shuddered, her eyes two big brown pools.

Iván swore, his face tense and angry. Not looking at her, he pulled at the long white ribbon at her throat and began to unbutton her blouse. Rachel lay quiescent in his arms, too exhausted, too full of pleasure at his touch to do anything to stop him.

'Sit up. I need a little co-operation,' he seethed.

Obediently, she sat on his knee like a reprimanded schoolgirl, her back straight, willing herself to stay upright. With a muttered imprecation, he opened the front of her blouse and the touch of his fingers on her burning skin made her groan aloud and throw her head back. Before she knew what was happening, the blouse had been ripped off, she had been flung on to the bed and he was tearing at her belt fastening, grabbing the zip and slipping her skirt down over her hips and thighs with such force and speed that she was left breathless.

His assault had changed somehow. Stupidly, she'd thought he was getting her to bed—helping her to undress. His rough handling had brought her to her senses. Or out of them and into another set of senses. For even in her half-conscious state, she both welcomed and feared what he was about to do. This was how it was, then, with a deeply passionate man. This was the way he took his women: arrogantly, confidently, as if he was driven to such raging desire that he had no time for niceties. It was the same technique as Alan's, but very, very different in reality, because she was so aroused that she wished her hands would obey her so she could help. Wild, hot floods of flame flowed over and through her, whether from his actions or the flu, she never knew. She was so bemused by what was happening that her head began to roll from side to side and she mumbled stupidly, longing for relief from her intolerable aching.

Trembling fingers on her suspenders made her draw in her breath deeply and let out a low moan again. But Iván was violent: ruining her stockings by catching them in impatient hands and peeling them off down to her toes, leaving marks on her delicate skin where his hands had scored pink lines as they thrust downwards. And then the stockings were free of her feet and some madness in her brain actually thought that his hands had skittered with the merest touch up her legs, pausing at her thighs and sliding away before they reached her emptiness.

Rachel was more aroused, more delirious than she had ever been in all her unfulfilled years of marriage. This was long-drawn-out torture of the most refined kind and she was aching with need. His eyes were stripping her naked with ruthless savagery. She moaned, her half-closed, misted eyes seeing pain and anger and desire flicker across his face.

His hands reached into the hot, damp hollow of her back and skilfully unhooked her bra, hurting her arms as he drew the straps down and eased her breasts from the lacy cups. Iván's breath surged fiercely in her ear as twin peaks, plump and cushioned, broke her vision, startlingly topped by hard, elongated nipples. She arched her back, unable to bear the burning between her thighs, longing for his expert release, for his mouth and tongue to assuage her desperate ache. Was she mad? Was she demented with fever?

He hovered over her, dark and inscrutable, only his eyes burning with a bright flame. Her hands had drifted up to shyly cover herself from his ravenous gaze, and then her eyes opened wide and frightened as she felt his hot hands at her briefs. His thumbs hooked into them expertly and a sharp tug exposed her heated skin to the air. The tiny triangle of blue lace was torn to pieces in his hands. Then she felt the sheets being pulled from beneath her body, and suddenly they covered her, completely covered her, from head to foot.

'Lie there,' said Iván thickly. 'Don't you *dare* get out! Don't move a muscle. If I see anything other than your head above those sheets when I come back, I'll thrash you. Clear?'

Rachel whimpered, bewildered, released from his ravishment, but imprisoned by her own desires. Crockery clattered in the kitchen, and then, once again, she became conscious of his brooding presence and forced heavy eyelids to open and look in his direction. Iván pushed back the covers and Rachel closed her eyes tightly, but he tucked his hands under her armpits and hauled her into a sitting position, plumping up cushions behind her head and back and settling the sheets demurely across her chest.

'Drink that,' he ordered, holding something hot and lemony in front of her nose.

'Iván,' she said huskily, her eyes closed, 'I'm...I'm all fuzzy.' She flung one hot arm above her head.

'Damn you!' he growled, his voice several tones lower than usual, as the words were drawn painfully from his body. This time, there was no underlying evil, only a raw, desperate longing. 'Mrs...Rachel, listen to me. You have a very high temperature and I'm afraid I shouldn't have given you that brandy. For God's sake, try to concentrate on what I'm saying. You've no idea what you're doing. Keep yourself *under* the bedclothes...' He tucked her in again and imprisoned her firmly by the tight sheets. '. . . and drink this. It will help you to sleep.'

Rachel finished the drink, forced to sip it down to the last drop by the domineering Iván. He removed the extra pillows and made her lie down.

'Go to sleep. Now!' he commanded.

'Yes, sir,' she said, feeling rebellious. It wasn't sleep she wanted at all.

From under drooping lids, her glance simmered. Iván's tie had been abandoned, his sleeves rolled up and the shirt unbuttoned further. That would be on account of the heat, she thought hazily. There was so much of his hunky body on show! With his habitually smooth hair ruffled, there was a sweetly vulnerable look about him. Like a vulnerable jaguar, she mused, with a sultry smile.

A small moan escaped her treacherous lips.

He looked at her with exasperation and drew the curtains, closing out the night.

'Sleep,' he ordered, leaving abruptly.

Rachel tossed and turned restlessly. Some time, perhaps in the early hours, she heard the sound of a shower running fiercely for a long time. Then someone walking around in the kitchen and clattering a kettle lid. Hot and feverish, she wandered in her mind, occasionally finding herself tangled in the bedclothes and having to struggle free.

The door opened softly and Iván's body stood blocking the doorway. Then something cool was caressing her forehead and she whimpered her pleasure. Her palms flattened against the hard, heaving wall of Iván's chest.

'Rachel! Stop that!' His voice cracked.

'Oh, I'm sorry,' she groaned. 'Forgive me. My head's in such a muddle.'

'You must rest,' he muttered. 'This is not good for you. It's not much good for me, either.'

'I ... I'm sorry to be a nuisance. I've put you in a very difficult situation. You must be so angry...' Furious, more like it, because she'd ruined his long-delayed reunion with his daughter. And now he was landed with a useless chauffeur, a demanding invalid!

The whole episode was filling her with deep shame. She dimly had memories of strong, atavistic urges that even now rippled treacherously through her body. 'I— I had no lunch, and the brandy...' Her head swam dizzily with the effort of speaking coherently. 'I can't...' Her brow puckered in frustration. Why wouldn't the words come out?

'It's all right,' said Iván quietly. 'Don't try to think. You can't help being ill.' The words sounded bitter. 'And don't worry that I had to strip you to get you into bed. I am quite aware, Mrs Wells, of the extent of your dislike for me. I am not offended; on the contrary, I admire your discrimination.' The cool flannel swept over her forehead, smoothing out the furrows. 'Now ... does that feel better?'

'A bit,' she whispered weakly. 'I have a horrendous headache.'

Delicate fingers gently massaged her temples. 'Shut your eyes and relax.'

How could she, when he was so close? There was the most astonishing, soothing sensation, building up inside her head. She was tired, dreadfully, unbelievably...

Exhausted, she slept heavily, right through to eleven o'clock the next morning.

'How do you feel?'

Rachel's lashes fluttered. Four men were definitely sitting on top of her body, and one of them had emptied a bag of grit into her eyes. Before that, he must have dried out her mouth with one of those sucking instruments the dentist used, and re-lined it with felt.

'Horrible,' she mumbled.

'Try some hot water and lemon.'

'Prefer prussic acid.'

'You've guessed,' he said drily.

Rachel opened one eye and gave him a sour look, but took the drink. It certainly helped to crisp up the felt lining. She leaned weakly back on the pillows, wondering at the ghastly sallow look on his face. Must be the designer stubble that had appeared, blackening his jaw and climbing up to the neatly shaped sideburns. Very sexy, like a Spanish bandit. Dear heaven, her fever was still drooling in her brain!

'I'm dying.'

'Funeral or cremation?' he asked in amusement.

Rachel's other eye opened and rested sulkily on his innocent face, with its raised, enquiring eyebrows. He beamed at her, with such a false 'jolly along the invalid' smile, that she began to giggle, jamming her face into the pillow in an effort to stifle the laughter, grabbing it and rocking backwards and forwards, as she heard his deep chuckle, too, infecting her with his merriment and its wonderful round tones, till they both eased off and sat, quietly shaking, then sighing with exhaustion.

'You can't be that bad,' he smiled, cupping his hand under her chin. 'Though I detected a note of hysteria there.'

'Yes,' she breathed, finding his beautiful, hovering mouth unbearably near. It had captured her eyes with its promising curves that seemed to be calling her... Rachel leaned closer, her eyes half-shut in desire.

'I don't believe you have the excuse of such a high fever this morning,' murmured Iván.

She smiled into his eyes, which had lost all their defensive barriers, and she could see almost into his soul.

'Rachel,' he breathed, his lips imperceptibly brushing hers. To her dismay, a frown creased his brow and he rose without looking at her any more.

Panic set in. What on earth had possessed her? He'd been temporarily drawn to her shameless hussy enticing and then immediately regretted it. Now what would he do? Visions of being thrown out for behaviour unbecoming to a chauffeur crashed into her fuddled brain.

'Where are you going?' she husked.

'Get my head seen to,' he growled.

His expression was ferocious. As he left, the telephone purred, and a few minutes later he returned.

'That was Tony,' he said, watching her reaction like a hawk. 'Wanted to know how you were. I told him you were in bed.'

'Oh.' She picked at the blue lace and pulled it high around her throat. The frightening Iván had returned, putting the other, nicer one to flight. If there ever was a nicer one; she'd probably imagined it.

'He asked if he could keep you company,' he continued in a flat tone. 'I told him you were probably infectious, very infectious.'

Her eyes flickered briefly at him, but he wasn't joking.

'He wanted to come down and take care of you,' said Iván coldly. 'Care for the love of his life.'

The old sarcasm was there, and Rachel flinched at its bite.

'I told him,' continued Iván relentlessly, 'that he'd be a damn liability as well as a damn idiot. I didn't want the two of you in bed down here.'

Rachel blinked in horror.

'Oh, I could hear the underlying lust,' he said with vitriolic pleasure. 'Mind you, he nearly bust a gut when

I said I'd stripped you and put you to bed. My ear-drums are just about recovering from the excess decibel level. It seems my brother has fallen badly. What *have* you been up to?'

The tone sounded vaguely enquiring, but that only thinly veiled the hard, tensile steel that lay beneath. Rachel closed her eyes wearily. Tony was taking too much for granted by talking like that, and Iván was rightly suspicious under the circumstances.

'No answer? Or don't you dare?' came Iván's soft, purring tones of persuasion. 'Perhaps you ought to know that I quizzed him. Gave him a touch of the Torquemadas, you know. Under pressure, he admitted that he's falling for you. Is that right?'

The hard steel had risen to edge his voice and also flashed in his eyes. Rachel, frail and far from calm, quailed at his hardness.

'How should I know?' she muttered. 'Please, I'm not well, my head . . .'

Two hands clamped around her upper arms in a bruising grip, snapping Rachel's head back in shock. Her beautiful hair flowed like a river over the pillow, spilling on to her naked shoulders and snaking over his fists.

'Don't take refuge in feebleness,' he said softly. 'What are you after? What is it that draws men to you, like moths to a flame? You're quite plain. You have an adequate body and fairly nice legs. Are you planning to spend your life marrying into families you work for? First Alan Wells, then Tony Latimer. A novel idea. You could call it car-hopping. In addition to trading in a new car, you also trade in husbands. Can't think why more women haven't thought of it.'

'No, you're wrong . . .'

'Really? Why is he so worried about *our* relationship, then? He's never bothered about my female employees before. And I'm beginning to wonder whether he's right to be worried. Are you covering yourself for all eventualities, in case Tony doesn't come up with a suitable offer? If you've set your bait for him, why spend half the night provoking me?'

Rachel had heard of people shouting quietly, and that was just what Iván was doing. He spoke in a near whisper, but what he said, the power held inside him, ready to burst like a thunderous explosion, denied that whisper and terrified her as much as if he had yelled at her.

'I—I didn't provoke you,' she said, remembering now with awful clarity what his touch had done to her and how her body had responded. He'd noticed. He would. He'd notice if one of her brain cells went on strike for half a second, so he'd certainly recognise a responding woman when he saw one. The memory made her eyes half close before she could stop them, and through her lashes she could see Iván's mocking disbelief, and then that annoying habit of his as he slicked the tip of his tongue to the corner of his mouth, leaving his lips soft and moist. Her hands flew to press down on her breasts protectively. He couldn't see under the sheet, but she knew—and somehow he did, too—that they betrayed her, swelling, hardening at the dark-stained tips as the warm tremors flowed through her body like mulled wine.

'You...didn't...provoke...me?' Each word was accompanied by an insulting sweep of his penetrating eyes over her highly tensed body, rendering Rachel a helpless, crumpled wreck, totally incapable of defending herself.

The shock, as he then abandoned her with a savage expletive, hit her like a slap in the face. He moved to the window, outlined in light. Rachel's sense of rejection sent her scuttling back into her shell. What a fool she'd been, she thought bitterly. Like a silly kid in primary school, admiring the excitement and aura surrounding the class wastrel. How could her standards have slipped so badly?

'I think you did,' he breathed raggedly, the eyes like burning coals in his suddenly gaunt face. 'I don't think you were as feverish as you made out. Certainly not this morning. Well, thank God I didn't take you up as the Dish of the Day. It had already been laid on a plate for another customer, hadn't it? And I can bet I know how he responded. As eager as a kid in an ice-cream parlour,' he sneered. 'Well, I'll ruin your plans in that direction. And, as for using me as a back-up, let me tell you, Mrs Wells, I don't take my brother's cast-offs, or his hopefuls. I take my own women. My own! God damn you to hell, I could beat you for being so crass!'

CHAPTER FIVE

RACHEL covered her face with trembling hands. She felt so humiliated, so horrified at the way Iván had twisted an innocent situation. And there was more. She had to acknowledge that she was upset by the truth. She *had* been deeply aroused by Iván; he'd known that, despite the fever, her real feelings had shone through, and therefore she had earned his scorn. That in itself was enough to shame her. In addition, if Cabinet Ministers quailed at the thought of being impaled on Iván's sharp wounding swords, then it wasn't surprising that her whole body trembled at his potential response.

'Take your hands away. I can't see your face,' he ordered.

'I'm not hiding, I'm trying to think straight! Please! My head's going round and round,' she wailed.

'I told you about Tony! I warned you!'

'*You* talk to him, then!' she cried, her eyes blazing. 'He's a grown man. I can't stop him saying whatever he wants. Tony and I got on very well. We're the same age and we have similar likes and dislikes. He was glad of a friend.'

'Friend! You are my *chauffeur*!' seethed Iván.

'I'm also a person,' she railed, 'and, if I happen to like Tony, I'm not going to pretend I don't just because he happens to be my employer's brother. I have to drive him too, you know. I can hardly slap his face and tell him to keep his distance. You *must* see what a difficult position I'm in! *You* convince him that I have a job to do!'

Rachel groaned and held her pounding head in despair. The brothers were only too ready to believe the worst about each other, and she was caught in the middle. It was a horrible situation.

'If you want me to resign, I will,' she said wearily, pushing back a silk curtain of hair that dropped over one eye. 'I'd rather throw myself at the mercy of the Job Centre again than be put through the Inquisition like this.'

'No! You can't... Don't resign.' Iván's poker face masked any of his thoughts. 'I need you. I'm sorry this has happened. Perhaps it *was* all Tony's fault. I'm sorry to have maligned you. Please forgive me; I jumped to conclusions. Tony's just been jilted, and I'm afraid he has wedding bells still ringing in his ears. I'll speak to him.' He looked down on her anguished face and frowned. 'You rest, and I'll bring you some lunch later.'

Rachel was left in peace. At least, that was the intention. As it so happened, she drifted in and out of drowsy sleep, wishing she could get her wildly rocketing emotions and thoughts in order. How could Tony think he was in love with her at this early stage? They hardly knew each other. And... She passed a perplexed hand over her forehead, trying to free the steel band that was tightening around her forehead. It had been astonishing how Iván had apologised abjectly, to stop her from walking out. It was almost as though he couldn't bear her to leave. Wishful thinking, she told herself. It was more likely that he found it hard to keep staff, and she was less irritating than most people to have around.

If only she didn't need the job so badly, she'd get out of this mess immediately. A self-derisory grin spread over her face. She might as well admit to herself that leaving Iván would be the hardest wrench in a lifetime of departures. No one would be as interesting to work for, or

as devastatingly attractive, dynamic, vital... The extraordinary thing was, he embodied everything she hated
in men: dark, over-assertive, heartless, crushing oppo-
sition ruthlessly... Tony embodied everything she liked.
He was blond, gentle, and not threatening. Her physical
reaction to the two brothers was vastly different: one left
her cold, the other heated her blood to fever pitch. More
dangerously, their minds linked. She sighed and gave
herself over to sleep. Her head was in too much turmoil
to make sense of her reactions, especially as they seemed
to be hell bent on personal self-destruction.

'I can do tinned soup and bread, or send out for a
pizza.' Iván's voice broke in on her dozing brain.

She flung a heavy arm over her face at the dazzling
light that hurt her eyes. Her skin felt hot, her mouth
tasted foul. She groaned.

'Soup or pizza,' he repeated remorselessly.

'Soup, thanks,' she croaked hoarsely.

'Go to the bathroom, wash and do your teeth. And
for God's sake, get a nightdress on.'

Rachel glowered at his retreating back, but did as he
had ordered and felt marginally better, though very weak.
It took her ages to move her leaden limbs, and she was
just opening a drawer to search for a nightie, when Iván
entered, carrying a tray.

'Hell!' In catching sight of her naked body, he'd spilled
some of the soup.

Rachel pulled out the first thing that came to hand,
and slid it over her head in hot embarrassment.

'I expected you to knock,' she mumbled.

'I'm trying to get used to the idea of being your
servant, but it's not a role that comes easily,' he growled.
'Get into bed. My God! Did you wear that kind of thing
when you were married?'

Crossly, Rachel stumbled to safety. She'd put on the thick brushed-nylon monstrosity that her mother-in-law had given her one Christmas. Well, it was too late to choose something more attractive. What on earth was she thinking? There was no earthly reason why she would want to look nice for this evil-minded flesh-gobbler!

That reminded her. 'I'm ravenous.'

'I didn't do too much. I thought the soup would be easier for you to manage in a mug and I cut the bread as thin as possible. Is it all right?' He eyed his efforts doubtfully.

'Yes,' said Rachel, startled that he should bother—and that he cared about her approval. 'I'm really hungry. I'm awfully sorry about this. I'll be OK from now on. I can look after myself. Aren't you having any lunch?'

'Mine's in the study. Eat that up. I want you on your feet as soon as possible.'

'Yes, sir,' she said meekly. Of course he wouldn't eat with her. What had she been thinking about? Still woolly-headed, she supposed. 'Thank you,' she said awkwardly.

'You'll pay me back,' he said in a softly menacing tone, 'I never give anything without expecting something in return.'

'No, sir.' Rachel lowered her eyes, her mind racing. She might have known! Goodbye overtime, hello one week of slave-driving.

Three days passed before Iván asked Rachel to drive him anywhere, and then for the rest of the week he spent his days in the office and his nights working late in the study. There were no assignations with women at all, and that didn't suit him. He retreated into a black cavern of silence. She was unhappy at his curt treatment of her, and spent long hours alone, trying to cheer herself up, without success.

Her spirits lifted on the following Friday afternoon as the Bentley glided along the narrow motorway to the farm. After days with a gloomy, morose man, it would be like a breath of fresh air to be in the country again.

Diana Latimer stepped from the house to meet the car. As Rachel opened the back passenger door, she saw that Iván's dark brows were drawn together, though his greeting was urbane as ever.

'Iván! How *awful* for you to have missed last weekend. We were desolate!'

'You might have been, Diana, but I'll bet my last penny that no one else was.'

Rachel shut the door quietly and looked up to see Tony bearing down on her.

'Rachel!'

Oh dear, Iván's not going to like this, she thought. Reluctantly, she faced Tony, but couldn't help smiling at his little-boy earnestness, the way his hair flopped so untidily. She was conscious of Iván and Diana watching in disapproving silence as Tony caught her arm, and his grey eyes smiled in welcome.

'You look pale,' he worried.

'I'm fine. Hello, Emily, Mike.'

'Where's Anna?' demanded Iván.

'You don't deserve to see the poor little lamb after letting her down so badly!' said Emily sharply. 'She...'

'Where is she?' hissed Iván, stepping towards her menacingly.

'Iván! Don't get so wound up,' urged Diana.

Emily snorted. 'Your daughter is hiding from you, behind my skirts, can't you see? Anna, come on, Daddy won't eat you.'

'That's a stupid thing to say!' Iván ignored his poker-faced daughter, and glared at his half-sister with accusing eyes before finally bending down to Anna. 'Come here, poppet,' he said softly.

In that abrupt switch from seething fury to gentle persuasion, Rachel recognised his hatred for Emily and his love for Anna. The child clutched at Emily's dress with tight little fists.

'Go on, he's not going to shout now,' encouraged Emily.

'Be quiet, woman! Stop feeding distrust into the child!'

At Iván's barely controlled fury, Anna had run back into the house. 'Oh, dear,' said Emily. 'After all my work! I *did* tell her you hadn't stayed away last weekend because you didn't love her...' She twisted her hands sadly.

'You silly little fool! I can see right through your scheming ways!'

'Iván, don't speak to Emily like that. She's doing her best,' defended Mike.

'Yeah,' he scorned. 'Her best to put seeds of doubt in Anna's mind. You must think I'm a simpleton, not to realise your game! I'm seriously thinking of taking Anna back.'

'No court in the country would put the child in your care,' cried Emily. 'She's obviously afraid of you...'

'That's your fault!'

'I keep telling her you're not as frightening as you seem.'

'Saints alive! Do you think that *helps*?' Pain was etched into Iván's face and Rachel wondered why he hadn't gone straight up to Anna, swept her up in his arms and magnetised her with his magical eyes. He should never have waited for her to come to him.

'Excuse me,' she said miserably, trying to escape this family row.

'Wait!' barked Iván irritably. 'You'll regret this, Emily. When I marry again...'

'You'd have to do better than chorus girls and secretaries to get Anna back,' cried the flushed Emily. Mike had tucked an arm around her shoulders. 'She's more my child than yours...'

'She's my blood!' growled Iván.

'She's terrified of you,' retorted Emily.

'Only because you fill her head with rubbish!' He raised agonised eyes to heaven and took several deep breaths. 'Why don't you adopt kids, as you said you would when I first signed the fostering papers? That would take the heat off the kiddie. You're too possessive. It makes me wonder if she wouldn't be better off with me.'

'Oh! You bastard! You wouldn't!' Emily was grey with shock.

'I've a good mind to ask you to leave,' breathed Mike, comforting his shaking wife.

'You wouldn't dare,' said Iván scathingly. 'In any case, I have legal access to my child and I intend to use that right. So, Mrs Wells, now you know a great deal about our family, don't you?' he said bitterly.

'Iván, you must behave,' warned Tony, 'or I'll get an injunction preventing you from coming here at all. It wouldn't be too hard.'

'No?' Iván's eyes narrowed. 'Try. I think you'll be sorry.'

The two men sized each other up silently; Iván scowling darkly, Tony knowing that his threat wasn't an empty one.

'You always cause trouble, wherever you are, just like your mother,' began Tony.

'By God!' thundered Iván. 'You push me too far!'

Iván's roar had made them all flinch. The jaguar was about to pounce, it seemed. Iván's hands were making fists, and there was a high colour on his cheekbones. His whole body seemed to be throbbing with a violent power that was ready to be unleashed.

'Please!' intervened Diana sharply. 'Stop this terrible quarrelling! I can't bear it!'

'I'm sorry,' Iván muttered. He stabbed a strong finger in the air at Tony. 'But he provoked me. He'll do anything to get me mad.'

'That's not too difficult. It must be hell, having your background.' Tony sounded smooth and innocent, but there was a light in his eyes that Rachel didn't like. She had to escape this awful scene. Iván was white with the effort of controlling his rage and his mouth was tightly drawn. In the impassive mask, only his eyes blazed a wild fury, and fierce pulses danced at his temples and, as he stalked into the house, Rachel realised that his pain was hers, that it hurt her to see him taunted so unmercifully.

'*Evil* man! Thank God he's not my brother. I think he skipped being a boy,' complained Emily. 'He'd understand his daughter better if he'd had a normal childhood, instead of running a stall in the Portobello Road at the age of eight, or whatever it was.'

Rachel digested this further evidence of Iván's extraordinary childhood with sadness. This family atmosphere was awful. It made her lonely life look quite appealing. As she walked towards the Bentley, to drive it around to the coach-house, Tony stopped her and pleaded with her to have dinner with them all. Conscious of Diana's disapproving eye, she hastily agreed, mainly to prevent his persuasion from becoming personal. His hands were already on her arms and she had to escape.

But how on earth was she going to stand a whole evening with everyone bitching at each other? And how could she bear to see Iván's tormented eyes? No wonder he slashed back at them with his vicious tongue; it seemed to be his only defence. Intentionally or not, Emily was turning his own daughter against him. If only she knew why Anna was the subject of a care order; it might tell her something about Iván's character. And suddenly she badly needed to know the truth about him. The evidence against him was damning, making him out to be heartless and vindictive. But something made her need further proof before she passed judgement.

Surprisingly, the meal was made pleasant because of two facts: everyone was very friendly, and Iván wasn't there. He'd had a tray sent to his room. A fit of the broods, as Tony so graphically described it.

That evening, Anna was withdrawn and uncommunicative, yet her whole demeanour was totally belied by the black, blazing eyes, which rested with a thoughtful intelligence on people when she imagined herself to be unobserved.

Rachel was conscious of Anna's scrutiny in the same way that she had experienced Iván's: they both searched deep within people, stripping away outer layers with a ruthless disregard for conventional social custom. As the family relaxed over drinks before dinner, Anna had eventually come to stand by Rachel's chair and touched her neat coil of hair, shocking Rachel with the similarity between the child and her father in the way she had lightly explored its silken weight.

A small hand stole around Rachel's neck, and Anna was suddenly sitting on her lap, dipping a small finger into the glass of Cinzano, while Rachel studiously ignored her. It was rather like acknowledging the presence of a nervous fawn, she thought afterwards, knowing that one false move might frighten her away.

The moment hadn't lasted long. Emily had murmured something about bedtime and whisked the suddenly sulky child upstairs. Rachel thought shrewdly that whenever Anna made any gestures towards anyone other than Emily, she was removed. Emily's love was understandable if she and Mike couldn't have children, but it still seemed over-possessive.

After the meal, Rachel took the short-cut back to the coach-house. It was a moonlit night, the moon a huge silver disc in the sky. Far down the grass walk lay the molten lead shine of the hammer pond, used by the ironmasters in Elizabethan times. Iván stood on the grassy bank, staring into the waters, a hard, remote figure, lonely, untouched by love. A deep feeling of sympathy washed over her. It couldn't be much fun having Iván's wild Latin temperament, being fed bitterness by your mother, seeing someone else inherit what you thought was rightly yours. Yet Iván had wealth. Why didn't he buy a place like this himself? Then he could have Anna with him.

Rachel sighed. That wouldn't be enough, would it? It had to be Latimer Farm or nothing. And Iván Lutero Posada didn't like being thwarted in his desires.

She oughtn't to waste her emotions feeling sorry for him. A lonely, stranded piranha was still a piranha, and even more deadly. It was when rivers dried up and reduced the amount of food available that piranhas were at their most deadly. But it was one thing to tell herself that, and another to put it into practice.

The next day, Rachel was an unwilling eavesdropper on another family row. Iván had taken the car and driven Anna to Drusilla's, the children's zoo in the country. She'd offered to drive him when he called for the keys,

but he'd refused curtly, and Rachel had the feeling that
he wanted his daughter all to himself. She was preparing
a snack lunch when she heard the Bentley draw up and
drive into the garage. Her windows on to the cobbled
courtyard were open, and she heard Anna's excited voice
with surprise.

'Lovely, lovely, lovely! My best day out, Daddy!'

'Hey, poppet!' Iván was laughing, and Rachel couldn't
prevent a peep out of the window. He held Anna high
in the air and she was squealing with delight. 'What did
you like best?'

'I liked the castle and I liked bouncing!' said Anna
breathlessly. Her little arms wrapped tightly around
Iván's neck as he lowered her down. 'Oh, and the slide
and the swings and the train...'

He grinned, a gleaming, heart-stopping grin, so rare
that Rachel hardly recognised him. So this was what a
happy Iván looked like! She couldn't tear her eyes away
at the sight of father and child, so content, so completely wrapped up in each other. A wave of longing
washed through her, paining her that she was excluded
from this happiness.

'Shall we go again, my darling?' he asked softly.

'Yes! Now!'

'Greedy! So, you've forgiven me for not coming to
see you? You understand why?'

'I do, I do,' she cried earnestly. 'I *knew* you were doing
something special. Rakle said.'

'Did she?' he murmured. 'You like Rachel, poppet?'

'Yes, I do. Can she come out with us sometimes?'

'Of course,' said Iván warmly, clearly unable to deny
his daughter anything. 'Now, we eat. After all that
climbing and balancing and bouncing, we both need
filling up.'

'Iván! What *have* you done with Anna? Look at her dress!' Emily ran up, a horrified expression on her face.

'I told you to put her in jeans,' he growled.

'She doesn't have any.'

'Well, she ought!'

'She's a *girl*!'

'Girls can be adventurous, as well as boys. I won't have my daughter in pink frilly things all the time.'

He put Anna down, and Rachel noticed how muddy and untidy the child had become. The pretty dress had withstood some drastic activity that morning! Anna looked confused, twirling a strand of hair and sucking it, her glance flashing between Emily and her father.

'What did you do, Anna? Did one of the animals push you over?' cooed Emily.

'We didn't have time for the zoo. We went to the Adventure Playground,' said Iván coldly.

'What? I told you she was too young for that...'

'Ridiculous! It was wonderful. You protect her too much. She enjoyed every minute.'

'Did you, Anna?' Emily sounded very stern.

'I—I——' she faltered.

'There! You frightened her again...'

'Christ!'

Emily grabbed hold of Anna and held her tight, crushing her face into her skirt.

'There, there, cherub,' soothed Emily. 'Emmy's here. You're safe now. Let's go and see if we can find a choccy biccy.'

'Christ!'

'I have asked you before, Iván,' said Emily, her thin mouth tight and angry, '*not* to swear in front of Anna. What Daddy said is naughty, cherub, you...' Her voice faded away, as she removed Anna from the infuriated Iván.

'God give me strength,' gritted Iván through clenched teeth. His head dropped to his chest, and a huge breath expanded his lungs. Then, every muscle in his body tensed, he turned and smashed a fist hard into the coach-house wall. Under the arc of his uplifted arm, the mask slid away to reveal misery and black despair. A terrible sadness poured into Rachel, blocking her throat with a hard lump and filling her eyes with tears. This, then was Iván's pain.

She was surprised that she shared his distress, and had felt a stab of knives in her heart as though they were twin souls. She supposed it was that unusual glimpse of the man behind the mask, a haunted, strained and helpless man, thwarted in his love for his daughter, a Goliath brought to his knees by a child.

Because he couldn't—or didn't choose to—look after Anna, she had become estranged, unable to know who to please when there was a conflict between her father and the woman she saw as a mother. If only he and Emily could work things out! It was ridiculous, tearing the child and themselves apart like this.

Rachel dropped back from the window, unable to watch Iván fight his demons any longer. He'd driven himself right into this situation and that must make it harder to accept. Iván was a very private man, who didn't show his real feelings very easily. It might be better if he did; people would sympathise with him more. The joyful man she had seen that afternoon, deeply content because a five-year-old child was happy, contrasted sharply with the man who hid inner agonies by sharp, rapier-like attacks on anyone who came near. If only she could tell him that people would like him more if he relented in his ruthless drive to appear invincible!

She was in little demand that weekend. Mike had driven the family to church on the Sunday morning in his own car, and they planned to take Diana on to her home in Brighton afterwards and stay for lunch. Rachel wondered whether to read her new paperback romance, but felt too restless. With everyone out of the house, it seemed a good time to take up Tony's suggestion that she should use the indoor heated pool. She'd decided against exposing herself in a bathing-suit when he was around, not liking to tempt providence.

All the exotic tropical plants and small palms made the pool room like a jungle. Stepping into its hot, moist atmosphere a little nervously, Rachel adjusted her classic-cut green Lycra suit and slid into the warm water, swimming off her distress and irritations. She floated peacefully, her long hair drifting around her like seaweed.

A splash disturbed the blankness of her mind and brought her upright, treading water and spluttering.

'Hi!'

'Tony! You're in Brighton!'

'Couldn't bear the idea. Didn't go.'

'But . . .'

'I fancied a short time alone with you.' He beamed at her and slipped a hand around her waist.

'No!' Rachel swam away, watching him with troubled eyes.

'Don't be unfriendly,' he pleaded. 'The atmosphere is ghastly. Diana's mad with Iván because he's been brooding and decided to go riding this morning instead of escorting her to church; Iván's impossible to speak to anyway; Emily and Mike are on edge because he's around; Anna's sulking, and there's only me being sane. And you. Tell you what, let's have a drink and chat.'

'Me and you? No, I——'

'Rachel, I must have some civilised company! Just you and me, chatting by the pool. What could be nicer?'

Rachel considered the situation warily, knowing she ought to refuse, but there were so many unanswered questions, and this could be her opportunity to straighten things out in her mind. Tony grinned at her face, knowing she was relenting, and slipped off for a bottle of wine. Dangling their legs in the warm silky water, and sipping wine, they chatted casually for a while, as Rachel tried to form her first question. But she was forestalled when Tony cleared his throat purposefully.

'Have you come to a decision about me?' he asked.

Her face registered caution. 'About what?'

'You tease!' He touched her cheek gently. 'I want to marry you.'

'Tony! I——' He was insane! What encouragement had she given him to think like that? Surely being friendly and getting on with someone didn't lead them to imagine there was mutual love?

'Bit quick, eh? Rachel, I've watched you while you've been here. You love Latimer's. You get positively radiant when we walk over the land. You're so calm and wistful, so elusive, that I have this overwhelming urge to care for you. When you were ill, I realised how much I was missing you.'

'But...' Rachel was stupefied. He almost sounded as if he meant what he was saying!

'Think about it and let me know tonight. I need to know quickly. I want us to marry as soon as possible.' Before she could stop him, he planted a quick kiss on her mouth. 'It's wonderful, having you around. In this hot desert of hatred, you're like a cool oasis. Can I come and see you after dinner, about nine? You can tell me your decision.'

'I can tell you now,' she began.

'No, do me the courtesy of thinking first. Latimer's could be yours, and your children's. Think of that. You'd be a rich woman, living in the country, with a loving family around you. Tempting? Think, Rachel. Let me know tonight.'

She gazed earnestly at his pleasant face, and decided that it would be better to let him down gently. He did seem very anxious and she didn't want to hurt anyone. 'Tonight,' she agreed quietly.

'I wish I didn't have to go now,' he said ruefully. 'But this is to be getting on with.' He caught her chin and kissed her, but all it was to Rachel was a contact of lips. 'I love you,' he smiled, apparently not noticing her lack of response. 'Must dash!'

Rachel followed his departure thoughtfully.

'My, oh, my!' drawled Iván. 'Haven't you done well!'

She swung around, startled to see him emerge from behind a palm tree. A hot flush of fury burned through her body, staining her skin. Another, stronger wave of heat coursed its inexorable journey. Iván was wearing an open-necked white shirt, the sleeves rolled high to his biceps, so that she could see the muscularity of the arms folded across his chest. His tight jodhpurs shockingly sheathed hard, masculine legs, and the high, slim black boots moulded to his calves, adding to the dominating, aggressive impression. His clothes fitted him like a second skin, leaving absolutely nothing to the imagination. Rachel was finding it particularly difficult to avoid the sight of his thighs and the embarrassing thrust of virility swelling the tight fitting jodhpurs.

Her heart thudded painfully and she scrambled to her feet, very conscious of her near-nakedness. The costume, so demure in Tony's presence, now was too high-cut in the leg, too low-cut at the front and back, and was fitting too smoothly over her breasts, hips and loins.

'I'm glad you have the grace to blush,' said Iván softly.

She didn't try to defend herself, but tilted her chin and began to move away, only to find he was blocking her path.

'So you weren't angling for Tony, eh? Yet you create a cool desert in a hot oasis? You prompt poetry from my naïve brother?'

'Please, let me go by,' she said quietly, clasping her hands to stop them trembling.

'A proposal in record time. Well done! Going to seal it tonight?' he mocked.

'There will be nothing improper,' she said stiffly.

'Cancel it,' he hissed.

'Certainly not! I'm prepared to work hard for you, but not to have my private time taken over!'

His eyes glinted dangerously. 'And if I demanded that you should drive me somewhere tonight?'

She sighed. 'I would drive you. That is my job. But it wouldn't stop Tony and me from getting together some other time, would it?'

'No,' he said thoughtfully. 'It wouldn't.'

Rachel shivered. Something within him had changed, making his eyes two fascinating black pools that drew her with their sensuality, so that she could not move when he stepped towards her.

He stood so their bodies almost touched, and she had to tilt her face to look up at him, bound by his awesome power to paralyse. He took a deep breath and his chest touched her body, bringing every inch of her skin alive. Rachel tried valiantly to keep breathing normally, knowing he'd mock her if her lips parted and she allowed the evidence of her desire for him to be seen. But he knew. He smiled, a knowing, triumphant smile, and taunted her with enigmatic eyes.

'Don't ever imagine you love Tony, will you?' he murmured. 'You have far too much love and affection to give to be saddled with a man who marries you in cold blood.'

Rachel's eyes lit up. His cruel words had released her from his deadly spell. 'Has it never occurred to you that he might be in love with me?'

'His desire to provoke me is greater and more deep-seated than any imagined infatuation,' he growled.

'Is there anything else?' she asked in an icy tone.

'Yes. Tonight you will tell him very firmly that you will not marry him.'

'Will I? We'll have to see,' she said sweetly. 'Sir.'

Iván's breath drew in noisily. Rachel took advantage of his apparent inability to control the situation to slip past. What she didn't know was that her stubborn words had gone too far. Iván was planning on taking drastic action.

CHAPTER SIX

RACHEL needed thinking space in order to handle this situation. Why on earth had she reacted so defiantly to Iván? She sighed. He did seem to have the capacity to make her mad! And she wasn't sure what game Tony was playing. Was he doing all this merely to annoy Iván? She wouldn't put it past him, the way the brothers disliked each other, and it was certainly getting the right results. Somehow she must find out, because it would make a difference to the way she refused Tony tonight.

Overwhelmed by the teeming thoughts in her brain, she chose to work out the ramifications of Tony's declaration as she walked. Walking was her panacea for all ills. It was very cold and blustery, so she bundled herself up in a thick turquoise jacket and a pair of tan cords, plaiting her hair into a thick rope to keep it out of her eyes.

Hands in pockets, walking slowly, she idled through the high, mellow brick walls of the kitchen garden, past the trenches of celery, the fresh green leaves breaking dark, fertile soil, the rows of beetroot and newly cut stems of globe artichokes. As always, pleasure swept over her to be in a garden. There was something very restful about the way plants calmly completed their cycles, ignoring the mess and chaos of the people around them.

Her fingers traced the decoration of one of the huge terracotta rhubarb pots. Her gaze swept the sheltered garden: everything in ordered rows, blackberries, apples, gooseberries and pears neatly trained and regimented. That was where safety lay: in methodical, wise hus-

banding of your resources. Wild Colombian renegades
had no place in her life, and it would be as well if she
realised that. Being with Iván was like being on one of
those awful rides at a fair, which whirled you around
first in one direction and then the other, apparently at
random, smothering you with a dark canopy and suddenly turning your world upside-down, at a speed which
left you breathless. Yet the ride was planned, there was
nothing haphazard or unsystematic about it at all. That
was Iván to a 'T'.

Rachel wandered on. The fig trees had been protected
from the frost with beds of straw around their tender
roots. That was what she needed—what she'd always
needed—a tender lover to protect her vulnerable nature.
On the surface, Tony was like that, but... She paused
at the arched gateway leading out of the kitchen garden,
and turned to survey it, and the beautiful farmhouse
beyond. It would be nice to live somewhere like this and
know it was yours.

She smiled sadly. The way she was going, she'd be out
on her ear in a day or so!

The fields and small copse ahead invited her. She'd
pick some holly and butcher's broom, and perhaps a
few snow-berries to brighten up her room. First, she'd
blow all the tension and troubles out of her head by
clambering over the stile and walking down to the small
lake.

The land she walked was owned by Tony, but she could
hear people ahead. Then, as she stood on the top step
of the stile, she saw them: Iván and Anna. He was
running at top speed, describing a huge circle, a bunch
of rose-bay willow herb in one hand. They were seeding,
and Anna squealed along behind him on her sturdy little
legs, her bright rainbow boots going like crazy as she
tried to catch the seeds streaming behind Iván like small

fluffy fairies. He completed the circle and caught her up, snatching her into his arms and swooping her into the air again. Then she appeared to be pleading, and Iván sat her on his shoulder and jogged in Rachel's direction.

He stopped dead in his tracks, a dark frown marring his face. Anna urged him on, her body rocking as if she was riding a horse.

''Lo, Rakle,' laughed Anna.

'Hello, Scrub.' Rachel could have bitten her tongue out as her pet name for Anna slipped out.

'We meet again.' Iván sat his daughter on the hanging bough of a tree near Rachel, and she pretended to gallop on it contentedly while he watched Rachel warily.

'Yes.'

'What did you call my daughter?' he enquired softly.

Rachel bit her lip. 'Scrub.'

'Explain.'

'We... Once or twice Anna and I have gone for a walk. I'm afraid we both get rather mucky and need a good scrub before she returns. We...' It sounded silly, looking into those dark velvet eyes and telling him, and she hesitated.

'Go on.'

'We stand at my basin and chant "Scrub, Scrub, Scrub-a-dub,"' she said defiantly, evoking a whoop from Anna.

'*Dirty* girls!' she cried in glee, exchanging a conspiratorial grin with Rachel.

'Sounds fun,' declared Iván. Rachel flashed a quick look at him, to see if he was mocking her, but his face looked perfectly open and extraordinarily approving. Then she remembered that anything defying Emily's pristine care of Anna would meet with his approval.

'Excuse me.' Rachel was about to walk past him and leave them to it, when a squeal from Anna made them both turn.

'Look at me!' she yelled excitedly.

Iván darted to stand guard beneath the bough, since Anna had decided it was much more fun hanging upside down on the branch.

'Is she all right?' asked Rachel anxiously.

'Don't you start,' growled Iván.

'Sorry.'

'Damn! Don't go,' he said quickly. 'Anna, my poppet, are we going fishing or not?'

'Oh, boy! Catch me!'

In complete faith, she launched herself off the tree and was deftly caught by her father, who slung her around his back.

'Will you come?' he asked Rachel.

'Yes, yes!' cried Anna, her black eyes dancing.

This was what Iván would look like, decided Rachel, if he was happy. She smiled her agreement and walked beside him. He was concentrating completely on Anna and her needs, mercifully releasing Rachel from any penetrating questions or that incisive gaze of his.

'...and that's where the deer have been eating the young trees,' he explained to his daughter.

'Mike shoots deer.'

'Does he?'

'And barsards.'

'Barsards?' puzzled Iván.

'Uhuh.' Anna dragged a spray of elderberries from a tree as they walked and stuffed them behind Iván's ear. 'Cos they take little girls away from their homes.'

Rachel sensed Iván stiffening.

'Tell me about these barsards,' he said softly.

'Mike's goin' to kill the barsard if he takes me away.'

'I see.'

His face had lost its mobility and shaped into a cold mask. Bastard. And Mike was referring to Iván himself.

'The barsard wants to be at my party,' continued the blithely ignorant child.

'How does he—it—know you're having a party?'

'It knows. So I'm going away.'

'But Anna, it's your birthday...'

The mask had gone, leaving naked despair, both in his voice and the drop of his mouth. Rachel felt a sharp, loving pain as his distress tore at her emotions. Why did people have to keep hurting each other? No wonder everyone built up barriers to deal with life!

'I know. Mike says the barsard isn't goin' to see me. You don't want it to hurt me, do you, Daddy?'

'No.' Iván's voice was agonised.

'Put me down! Put me down! The lake!'

He watched Anna run to the small pond and search in the undergrowth for a stick suitable to use as a fishing-rod. Iván tied some string and a paper-clip on to it and she paddled happily in her boots, stopping every few moments to investigate something in the shallow water. Iván watched her gloomily.

'I—I'd better go back,' said Rachel, feeling she was superfluous.

'Prefer Tony's company?' he snapped. 'Oh, I'm sorry. Forgive me, that was unnecessary. I'm a little sensitive at the moment.'

'I thought you'd rather be alone with your daughter,' said Rachel quietly.

'My daughter? Or Emily's? How do *you* see her, Rachel?'

'She's yours, of course. Look at her, her hair is as black as yours, and it's got that blue sheen on it, too. She's tough, quite beautiful, as wary as hell, very intelligent and terribly sensitive...oh!' She put a hand to her mouth in horror at what she'd been saying.

Iván threw her a mocking look. 'Steady, you'll ruin my reputation! No one has accused me of sensitivity before.'

'That doesn't mean to say it isn't there, does it?' she retorted.

'There are times, Rachel,' said Iván, fixing her with a sombre stare, 'that I feel...' He broke off and bit his lip. 'Sit with me for a moment,' he invited, patting a tree-stump.

I'm obeying because he's my boss, Rachel told herself. And because I'm terribly sorry for him. If he knew that, he'd probably be insulted and retreat behind scathing remarks. Barriers lay between them: their working relationship, her natural reserve and his tough, self-sufficient image. Yet now, she would have described him as forlorn. It would be nice to cradle his sleek head against her breast, soothing his deep wounds. Nice? It would be hell! He was beginning to reach parts that no man had reached before. For heaven's sake, she *couldn't* feel tender and protective towards a man like Iván Posada! You didn't cuddle ravenous jaguars or hungry piranhas!

'You like it here?' he asked, alerting Rachel to the way he had been watching her intently for the last two minutes.

'I love it,' she enthused, channelling her emotions into a safer area. 'I walk as much as I can each day. It's very calming.'

His eyebrows rose fractionally. 'So you need your passions cooling, too?'

Pity she'd forgotten how sharp his brain was. 'Occasionally I am irritated about something,' she said.

A slow smile curved his lips. 'Of course. You don't have passions. Well, I don't mind admitting to mine, and pretty grim they are sometimes, too. Once I even caught myself wishing I was as placid as Tony. Can you believe that? I must have been as depressed as a hangman who can't tie knots.'

Rachel tried to hide her involuntary laugh, wishing his humour wasn't always so black. 'Anna loves it here,' she said, without really thinking. Her main aim was to lighten the conversation.

'Hmmm. She'd love it more if Emily allowed her to come home grubby. It's only with you and me that Anna discovers there's a world beyond the nice clean pavements and shopping precincts,' he said sourly. 'My father and I always spent the little time we had together out here. Has Tony told you my story?' he asked, with a cynical twist of his mouth.

'About your mother, and the family refusal to accept you as a Latimer?' she said quietly.

'My mother fought for years to get me the Latimer name. My father, Philip, knew I was his son. He knew how much my mother loved him.'

'But Tony said . . .' She stopped at the savage look on his face.

'I can imagine,' he said in a low whisper. 'He calls my mother promiscuous. He got that from Grandfather Latimer. But it isn't true! And one of these days I'll clear her name. She's remained true to her first love and never looked at another man.'

Rachel was silent, trying to understand why Tony should revile Teresa Posada. 'If you were accepted as Philip Latimer's son, would you inherit the farm and the land?' she asked suddenly.

'No. You see, my father's will had left everything to me and Teresa, as some recompense for the misery we'd suffered and our struggle to make ends meet. The only trouble was, that he died before my grandparents did. So they still owned the farm, the shares, the bonds, the gilt-edged securities...' His voice faded into a helpless sigh. 'They loathed the idea of my mother and me being accepted as family, and made damn sure we weren't included in *their* wills. When they died, Tony inherited.'

'You went to your father's funeral, I understand,' said Rachel, remembering the fuss he had caused. It was understandable, if inexcusable.

'Yes. Did Tony tell you how we were treated?' he asked in chilled tones. 'How mother was manhandled the moment she stepped from my car, by two thugs? The Latimers certainly know how to make people feel unwanted,' he said bitterly.

'Tony said...' It had been a different tale. Who was right? Or perhaps they both were, with different viewpoints.

'Tony can't be trusted. Do you honestly think either of us would deliberately set out to make a scene at the funeral of the man we loved? We were far too upset. Where do you think I got this, if not in defending my mother?' He ran an angry finger over his scarred cheekbone and broken nose. 'I'll never forget that terrible, humiliating day, as long as I live!'

Miserably, Rachel fiddled with her coat buttons, staring into space. Who should she believe? She knew who she wanted to believe, but was she letting her emotions overrule her head?

'Has he told you why he has to marry so soon?' he asked suddenly.

'I beg your pardon?'

'Rachel, if Tony doesn't marry by the end of this year, everything goes to a cousin we've never even seen, who's the nearest male heir. There's been an entitlement on

Latimer wealth since the seventeenth century, when the estates were nearly lost because of some woman-hater. He was finally persuaded to marry when his father locked this requirement into the inheritance. Any Latimer heir, unmarried by the age of twenty-five, forfeits his right to the estates. Tony's motives, you see, are questionable.' His eyes searched her face minutely. 'God! Do you think I'm joking?' he asked bitterly. 'He does this every time.'

'Every...'

'You're not the first woman he's proposed to, by any means.'

'You're trying to make me think badly of Tony,' she said in confusion.

'It's true. Ask him,' said Iván coldly. 'He wants a wife, Rachel, a wife in a hurry.'

'I think he might love me,' she said quietly, not at all sure.

'He doesn't love you in the way that... that you want to be loved,' he said savagely. 'You can't seriously be considering his proposal!' His hand grabbed her wrist and held her prisoner, the fingers biting cruelly into her tender flesh. 'You won't!'

'Let me go!' she cried. 'You're confusing me, between the two of you, and I have this terrible feeling that you're both using me for your own selfish ends! Besides, what happened to the other women he proposed to? Did they turn him down?'

'I... persuaded them to, yes,' said Iván softly.

So it was pure vindictiveness that made him forbid her to accept Tony's proposal. A look of pure distaste curled Rachel's lip. Her scathing eyes met his and, for the first time since she'd known him, he broke the link by looking away, unable to accept her scorn. Without another word, she coldly withdrew her hand from his lifeless fingers and quietly strolled away, her head held high.

There was a small splash and she half turned to see that Anna was sitting down in an inch of water, patting the surface with the palms of her hands. Iván was squatting beside her, stroking her hair absently, not minding that her little jumpsuit was soaked. Emily would probably go mad when the kiddie returned.

Anna needed someone around who wasn't paranoid, who was a balance between the neat and tidy Emily with her limited ideas of what a girl could do, and Iván, who took a perverse delight in making his daughter behave unconventionally. She would have liked to help Anna, but once she had rejected Tony she didn't see how she could stay as Iván's chauffeur—it would be too embarrassing. A coiling ache twisted in her stomach. She would have to leave Iván. She didn't know whether to hate him or love him, but she did know that she'd be lost without him. Seeing him so happy with Anna had made her long to reach that well of tenderness beneath the barricades he had erected to protect himself from any further agony.

When Tony came, she'd find out soon enough if Iván was telling the truth. And she must ask about Anna's tale that her father was to be excluded from the birthday treat. Perhaps the child had misunderstood. She hoped so. If not, there was more malice in the family than she'd thought. Unravelling this web of deceit was going to be difficult, but she owed it to herself to know exactly who was deceiving whom. At the moment, she didn't trust any of them.

At half-past seven that evening, she began to chop some fresh vegetables for a light supper. Tony was due at nine and that would give her time to eat, clear away and watch the serial she was following before he arrived.

Her hand nearly slipped and cut a finger off at the sharp rap on her door. Glancing at her watch, she wiped her hands on her apron with a sigh. Tony was an hour and a half early! And she looked a mess. Her hair wasn't up yet, it was tumbling wildly around her shoulders.

'Come in,' she called. 'It's not locked, Tony.'

Her smile of welcome died on her lips as Iván stepped in, dark and handsome in a dinner suit. He was cold, immaculate, implacable. If that had been Tony, she mused, his hair would have been awry and probably some of his shirt would have come untucked from his trousers.

'Yes?' she said sharply.

His eyebrows rose enquiringly. 'What exactly are you saying yes to?' he murmured in his deep, rich voice.

Irritably, she whirled around and chopped the mushrooms unnecessarily, going more carefully with the chef's knife when she sensed Iván was immediately behind her. A tense heat electrified the air, warning her that he was very close. She reached for a red pepper and sliced it carefully.

'Is there something you wanted, sir?' she asked coolly.

'You could say that,' was his laconic reply. 'Got any drink?'

'In the larder.'

'Is that your supper?'

'Yes.'

'Looks good. I haven't eaten. Can you spare some?'

He was ruining her evening! Iván was the last person she wanted to spend time with. 'You wouldn't enjoy it. I'm only stir-frying vegetables.'

He checked over the pile of chopped carrots, broccoli, cauliflower, potatoes, peppers and mushrooms. 'Very healthy. That will do nicely, thank you.'

Drat! Rachel poured olive oil into the pan.

'I did you a drink, since you're not driving,' he murmured into her ear.

The whisper of his breath made her flinch with its intimacy. She really must get a hold on herself. The impulses that leapt between herself and Iván were switched on and off at his will, and she would *not* let herself be dominated by his sexual potency. She wasn't like all the other women, who fell for him like ninepins. She had high principles.

Iván's hand was rock-steady as he handed the glass to her. It didn't leave the glass, and their fingers touched, trembled, and separated.

'So,' murmured Iván, slinging his jacket on to a chair and drawing up a high kitchen stool, 'are you going to stay with me as my chauffeur?' He swung his leg indolently and laughed gently as her eyes dropped to watch the muscles expanding and contracting in his thigh under the stretched material of his black trousers.

'Probably not,' she said with a frantic attempt to calm her thudding heart and deny the sexual challenge that poured out to her. She drained the vegetables and tipped them, golden-brown and temptingly crisp, on to two plates.

'I see. This looks very good.'

Rachel placed the plates on the table and he brought the drinks over. 'Please sit down, sir,' she said courteously.

A wry smile touched his lips. 'Why leave, Rachel?'

'Personal reasons.'

Iván watched her over his glass. 'Tony?'

'I really can't discuss it, Mr Posada,' she said pleasantly, keeping her eyes on her food. There was a terrible empty hollow in her chest at the prospect of leaving him.

Iván had stopped eating. 'What would persuade you to stay?' he asked huskily.

Startled, Rachel looked up and knew immediately that it was a terrible mistake. Iván's eyes locked with hers, searching deeply, searing her with hot desire and a deep longing. Her breathing quickened. The room was completely silent except for the thudding of her heart. Still he held her, enthralled, trapped. Indirectly, Iván had warned her about this. He was persuading her to refuse Tony in the only way he knew how. He intended to seduce her to spite his brother, and she was on the brink of welcoming his persuasion!

Slowly, Rachel stood, and Iván rose too, his eyes never leaving hers.

'You fool,' he breathed. 'You blind, misguided fool! Don't you ever listen to your instincts?'

'I have too much sense for that,' she said shakily.

'And when you meet someone whose very presence sets your pulses racing? When every part of you comes alive? What then, Rachel?' he growled. 'What if a small gesture...' his eyes fastened hungrily on the way she pushed back her long hair, wavy from its plait '... becomes so erotic to you that you could almost groan aloud in the need to satisfy the ache it creates?'

His tongue hovered in the corner of his mouth, and Rachel found herself breathing so shallowly that she was becoming dizzy.

She backed away till her back came into contact with the wall. That was it; she had nowhere to go. Iván prowled menacingly towards her.

'Iván——'

'Ah, Christian-name terms, now you're almost one of the family, eh?' he taunted, thudding both palms on the wall either side of her head.

His chest and shoulders heaved alarmingly; his face was blazing with a wildness. Rachel tilted up her chin in defence and tried to prevent him from seeing her fear.

'You are extraordinarily beautiful, Rachel,' he said with a dangerous huskiness.

'Don't be ridiculous.' What a stupid remark! She was perfectly well aware that he couldn't find her in the least bit attractive, but the words nevertheless raged in powerful flattery through her brain. To her fury, heat had leapt within her, scorching her throat and making her speech croaky. He'd imagine he was succeeding!

Iván's hand strayed to her face, and then he threaded his fingers through her hair. 'Your eyes are as deep and as dark as a mountain tarn,' he murmured. 'And your skin...' His fingertips skimmed her forehead, sensitising the small hairs between her brows, trailing down her straight nose and curving along her cheekbones. '...it's so soft and smooth it could almost be porcelain.'

'Don't touch me!' she gasped, hating his deception, hating herself for wanting to be deceived.

'You need to be touched.'

As he pushed his fingers over her scalp, Rachel almost groaned aloud at the sensation. She could feel the warmth of her head in contrast with his cool touch, and wondered why her hair seemed to be springing into energised sensitivity merely because he touched it.

'You fabulous creature,' he said thickly.

Rachel darted an anguished glance at his face. His eyes were filled with carnal desire, shining with a predatory gleam. The jut of his nose seemed more arrogant, more severe, with a pagan flare to his nostrils. Then there was his mouth: curving sensually, his teeth a white slash in his face as he grinned in pleasure. Iván Posada had never looked more like a passionate male animal than he did now, and Rachel had never been more afraid of a man in her life.

Or of herself.

'Want me to kiss you?' he asked.

'No, I do not!' she said shakily. It had been intended as a denial. To her ears, the words sounded uncertain.

Iván took a step closer. Now their bodies were almost touching and Rachel was horrified to find that her breasts strained in the soft golden shirt till she *was* touching him, and that she was having to press her hips hard against the wall to prevent them from thrusting forwards, too.

Instead, it was he who moved his pelvis slightly, the contact of his thighs unnervingly powerful and insistent, destroying every shred of fight left in her.

'So erotic. So seductive.' Gently, he shifted imperceptibly from side to side. It was enough to tease the peaks of her breasts, and he knew it. It was enough to make her catch her breath at the sheer force of his masculinity teasing her thighs so skilfully.

'Don't you like men kissing you?' he murmured.

She was hypnotised by his mouth. 'I——' She swallowed and cleared her throat nervously. 'It's so much nicer being kissed by someone you love,' she declared.

'*Nicer?* Who wants *nicer*?'

His body slammed hard against hers so that she felt the hardness of every muscle. Every one. Why had no one else felt like this? she wondered wildly. Iván was so...searingly aroused. She caught his eye. He was watching her like a hawk, his flickering eyes reading every emotion. Then, as her hands tried to slip between the shocking intimacy of their bodies and push him away, his head swooped, taking her lips in ruthless possession. Again and again his mouth plundered, burning, tearing into her senses with a wild, raging passion. Her stiffened, taut body could only melt beneath such an onslaught, and it surrendered, despite the outrage in her mind. And then that, too, dissolved as Iván's mouth coaxed open her lips and his tongue began to thrust suggestively, while his hands slid from the wall and relentlessly explored her body with rapacious eagerness.

'You will never forget me, do you hear?' he rasped. 'Every touch, every kiss you have ever received will be wiped out, and all you will remember is me. And...this...and this...my kisses...my mouth... tongue...' His teeth sank into her lower lip and savaged it gently, giving Rachel the impression that he could tear her limb from limb if she resisted.

She was frightened, bewildered by her reactions, but he didn't give her time to consider them. His mouth, hands, tongue, even his body, were moving with incredible sensuality, not giving her a chance to think, to rationalise, to react calmly or sensibly.

'God, you're exciting!' he muttered through his teeth, barely able to control himself. He scooped her up and laid her on the floor by the log fire. Before she could protest, his powerful body lay across her and a multitude of kisses landed on her face, hot and moist, soft and hard, all at the same time, gentle, yet undeniably passionate. Within the circle of his lips, her own mouth emitted a low moan and, as it did so, their tongues meshed.

Iván shuddered throughout the length of his body, creating such a love-pain in Rachel's heart to find this one unguarded response from her could affect him so deeply. He shifted his body, grinding fiercely against her loins. The heated column that heralded his desire so powerfully, also warned her of his utterly selfish, animalistic intentions.

'Yes, yes, you need me too, don't you?' he whispered, his breath hot and ragged, making her shiver with anticipation.

'I don't. There's no love. How could I want you?' she moaned.

Iván's lashes lowered over sultry eyes. His hand swiftly undid the top two buttons of her blouse, and Rachel dug her nails into his biceps as his raiding mouth devoured her neck. A warm savagery shook her limbs as he drew on the skin there. She wriggled her body like an eel to escape, but his weight was too great and his legs merely spread across hers. By the pressure of an increased heat against her loins, his frantic mouth and throaty groans, her writhing was inciting him unendurably.

'Don't fight me, Rachel. I need you.'

At his throaty cry, an aching need engulfed her and, fully conscious though she was that all he wanted was relief from his highly sexed appetite, nevertheless that cry sank deep into the tender heart of her, recognising that men like Iván didn't normally expose their slipping control so readily.

'Let me love you,' he whispered, his mouth suddenly gentle, lingering sweetly at the pulse in her throat. 'Things have gone too far. I can't hold back any longer. I've never felt so completely incapable of coherent thought before.'

Rachel dearly wanted to be convinced. The power that this wild, untamed and cynical man claimed she exerted, totally awed her. Her self-control was hanging by a thread. It needed only the smallest of triggers to snap that thread, the slightest touch on her ragged emotions, and he knew it. But it was a risk, and the consequences of that could be great. She longed and feared for its success.

His fingers lightly stroked her temples, while her mouth trembled appealingly beneath his, tempting, womanly, innocent.

'Rachel, I want to show you every delight I know, to lie sated in your arms, and arouse you again and again till you're in a ferment of impassioned longing. Love me,' he husked, permitting his desire to be heard. 'I need to possess you. So very, very badly.'

Rachel's fragile defence was expelled in a rush of air as she let out all the breath from her lungs and found the reason for the strange, dark attraction that existed between herself and this man who was so encased in a protective shell that nothing could penetrate it, except love. And she wanted to be the one who found him, released him. Giving herself would open the doors that had lain shut, because he might give, too. She had a whole life of love to lavish on someone, and knew that Iván could absorb all that and demand more. Like her, he longed for love, and she could give that. What if he couldn't give love himself? Did it matter?

Her hands reached up to cradle his head, to encourage him. They locked into his strong, springing black hair, and as his mouth ravaged further she dragged his head up.

'Such passions! Who, but I, would have believed it?' he asked softly, claiming her mouth in a sweet kiss. He left her for a moment, and switched off the light, so that only the glow of the log fire fell on her. With a swift gesture, he stripped away his tie and flung it away, then half lay across her, supporting himself by his hands.

'Undo my shirt,' he commanded gently. 'I want you to touch my body. Feel my warmth, my strength. It's all for you, Rachel.'

Her hand refused to obey and he shifted his balance, lifting her fingers. As if in a dream, they undid one, two, three, four buttons, before her nerve failed.

Iván's torment glowed like coals of fire beneath hooded eyes. 'For God's sake, touch me!' he muttered.

Wonderingly, her hand slid inside his shirt to that warm, golden chest, lightly travelling over the pure silk of his skin and the crisp hairs. She lifted her head a little and buried her face in the hair, nuzzling it and offering small kisses, tasting the maleness of his body and the wiriness of the hairs. Entirely of their own volition, her teeth began to tear gently at his chest, then her mouth circled each nipple in turn. His eyes watched her, his tongue moistening his lips wickedly.

'Learn me,' he whispered. 'Learn every inch. Slowly.'

Her fingers slid into the strong column of his throat, along the silk that covered a steely jaw, and traced the dark sideburns, first one and then the other. His jaw tightened, and they shared gentle glances. He was telling her something, but her drugged brain refused to operate. All she knew was that she was intensely aroused and intensely in love. This time, though, she was being promised complete satisfaction. Iván would know how to please her. She was already on the edge of fulfilment.

She tore away the last few buttons, ripping them from the material.

'Me, too,' she breathed. 'Learn me. I ache inside for you, Iván.' Her invitation made him groan.

'I can take away that ache, my darling, mine, too. It may take a long, long time, but we'll get there, eventually, I promise you that. God, you're the most exquisite creature I've ever tasted!'

'I hate to hear about your other women,' she moaned.

'Forget them. They're nothing. They've always been nothing,' he soothed. 'This is real. Give yourself to me, Rachel. I want *everything*.'

How savage and tender his eyes were! Quivers of fear at his power ran through her body. The blood pounded in her ears as the dishevelled Iván placed both hands tenderly on either side of her head, and his kiss was delivered with incredible meaning. Her eyes closed and she was aware only of her heightened sense of touch, her brain registering his mouth, the slight brush of his nose on her cheek, his uneven breathing tingling each hair of her skin. Then her brain alerted her to the insistent pressure of his knee as it parted her legs, thrusting up against her writhing pelvis as he captured her mouth again and again in raiding swoops, with all the assurance of a man who knows his destination and is almost there.

Her hands were pushing his shirt off his shoulders frantically, and for a moment she thought he had drawn back to slip it off, but then his hands released the side of her head and she could hear clearly again. Her horrified eyes widened when she realised it wasn't Iván's husky tones that invaded her consciousness, but Tony's voice, bordering on hysteria.

CHAPTER SEVEN

'GOD, you're *unspeakable*! Leave her alone, or I'll...'

'You'll what, Tony?' growled Iván, still hovering above Rachel. She tried to struggle up, but Iván pressed her down again. 'Stay, my darling. He'll be gone in a minute.'

Her mouth opened in astonishment.

'I'll kill you!' yelled Tony.

'You and whose army?'

'Tony!' Rachel's cry was stopped by Iván, bruising her swollen lips.

'Don't draw away from me, Rachel,' he mumbled into her mouth. 'For pity's sake...'

Something heavy pressed down on Iván, crushing her, and then he slid away, rolling on the floor with Tony. But Iván smoothly escaped from Tony's flailing, frantic attack, and stood up, brushing down his trousers, an inscrutable expression on his face.

Rachel took one look at his disarrayed hair, the torn shirt and naked torso and shut her eyes in despair.

'Outside,' Iván said softly to Tony.

Tony gulped and stayed on the floor, shaking. 'You swine! You arranged this, didn't you? This seduction was intentional!'

Iván's eyebrow rose sardonically. 'Of course it was,' he said in a low growl. Rachel closed her eyes in humiliation and horror. He was more cruel and ruthless than she'd ever imagined! 'If I hear,' he continued, 'that you're trying to get too friendly with Rachel ever again, you'll find more than one Latimer can get his face smashed!'

'Iván!' Rachel was frightened at the savagery in his eyes. He meant every word.

Tony was white with shock. 'You're hell-bent on ruining my life, aren't you?' he breathed. 'Rachel is just one more notch on your bedpost.' His accusing eyes swung to Rachel. 'I don't know what he's told you, but he says the same kind of thing to every woman, don't you realise that? He pretends to every one that they've succeeded in capturing his heart. Oh, how could you be fooled by this man?'

'I——'

'Don't listen!' snapped Iván. 'He's lying. Trust your feelings, Rachel. You and I are very much alike.'

'Never!' Rachel was shocked at the very idea.

'Yes. Both illegitimate, unhappy childhoods, no love, early and disastrous marriages, and...' his voice dropped to a lower register '...totally uncontrollable, primitive passion.'

'No!'

Iván held out his shirt to her in evidence, then pushed the material off one shoulder and deliberately exposed the red marks scored by Rachel's nails.

'You evil bastard!' cried Tony. 'She was fighting you...'

'Fight? A love fight. Shall I show you how she attacks me?' he murmured.

Rachel scrambled up, her eyes blazing.

'Look how she trembles,' he continued, raking her body with longing eyes and sending flames leaping into her womb.

'That's fear!' spat Tony. 'She's afraid of your potential violence.'

'She's afraid of her own boundless sexuality and the fact that I can arouse it,' he replied darkly.

Rachel's bones melted down to her toes. 'I——' Darn it, couldn't her brain crack out anything more than that one word in her defence?

'I love you, Rachel,' said Tony, his grey eyes haunted.

'I've told her why,' growled Iván. 'I've explained why you're so ready to love.'

'My God!' breathed Tony.

'Is it true?' asked Rachel hoarsely.

'About the inheritance? Yes. But I *do* love you. And every time I've been near finding some happiness in my life... *Stop mocking*, you bastard!' he yelled as Iván laughed mirthlessly, '...every time, this—this devil incarnate has turned my girlfriends away from me by his lies and manipulative scheming. But you! I never expected you'd fall for his smooth talk!'

'Oh God!' wailed Rachel. 'Will you both get out of here? I don't ever want to see either of you again!'

Her past, present and future had congealed into one solid, nasty lump. She had no job now, because of the warring brothers, no home, no prospects. She was almost beside herself with despair at the unkind way Fate had treated her. She refused to think how close she had been to giving herself to Iván, and how brilliantly he had deceived her. It was something she didn't want to face. The truth of her feelings was far too painful.

'Rachel, I still want to marry you!' cried Tony.

'No! Never! Get out, both of you!'

'Damn you to hell, Posada!' fumed Tony. 'Rachel, don't let this spoil things between us. Look, if it makes you feel better, you need never see him again. This is my land and I can throw him off it if I please.'

'Not on your own, you can't,' said Iván unpleasantly.

'I'd call the police. I'm not such a fool to tangle with vicious psychopaths. I'm tired of putting up with your vitriolic remarks. Clear out! You'll have to meet Anna elsewhere.'

'You bastard,' said Iván softly.

'Please, Rachel,' insisted Tony, 'you owe it to me to hear what I have to say.'

'No! I've had enough! I'm leaving in the morning, getting out of your sordid, nasty lives. I always wanted a family of my own, but if this is what it's like, I'm glad to be alone!'

'I'll never let you go!' cried Tony.

With an impatient snarl, Iván grabbed hold of his half-brother and frog-marched him out, leaving Rachel shaking and upset. Distractedly, she picked up the barely touched plates of food and scraped them into the pedal bin. Then a violent rage took hold of her; she held both plates aloft and smashed them to the brick floor. It seemed they represented the destruction within her. And it had been all Iván's fault, she thought angrily. He'd deliberately woken her passions and desires after she'd so successfully subdued them.

Tony was offering to make her dreams come true. A nice, pleasant, kind, fair man. A nice, even marriage with nothing to ruffle its surface. That was what she had looked forward to, ever since she'd divorced Alan. But the reality didn't appeal. God help her, she longed for the wild fury of a man like Iván, the hasty fingers, unable to wait a decent interval while she carefully undid her clothes, the halting, incoherent, uncontrollable phrases that told her she was exciting him beyond all his shaky control.

It was madness. Infatuation. She had to break free from all of them, even if this meant bitter hardship and a broken heart.

With resignation, she cleared up the broken china and prepared for bed. Two sleepless hours later, she rose, padded along the gallery in the dim moonlight, poured herself a hot toddy to help her relax, and allowed the alcohol to weaken her bones. Better. She'd drop off in no time. Relieved, she clambered into bed again.

Tingling sensations spread through every muscle and sinew. A warm mouth slid over hers. Stunned, she slowly raised her lashes to meet black, glittering jet.

'Rachel!' His voice shook with emotion.

'Get out!' she moaned. Frantically, she began to struggle, but Iván's hard body lay heavily, one hand lifting her head to his mouth and the other feeling for the bedclothes, then pushing them impatiently away, drawing down the thin straps of her nightdress and covering her rising breast.

A shudder tore through him as her nipple surged between his fingers. Rachel managed to free one hand and pushed ineffectually at his shoulder, so warm and golden in the half-light. So smooth. His mouth was doing the most wonderful things, his fingers, his body... Rachel writhed with an involuntary movement, arching her body into his.

'I couldn't leave you. I can't let you go out of my life. I couldn't forget... Oh, Rachel, I'm obsessed by you!'

Madness! One minute she hated him, the next... God! How could she keep sane while he...? Seduction, revenge; that's what drove him. Not *her*. He cared nothing for her as a person, or even as a mistress, she thought coldly.

'You deliberately and cold-bloodedly tried to seduce me!' she seethed. 'You even had the nerve to admit it!'

'Deliberately and hot-bloodedly,' he murmured, his breath thrilling her sensitive ear. 'I've wanted you for so long, ached for too many nights. I couldn't wait any longer.'

'No, Iván!'

'Yes, yes, yes, my darling. Every fibre of my being fits with yours. We have to become one person or we'll be unhappy and incomplete.'

That wasn't Iván talking, it sounded like some crazy romantic fool... 'I——'

'How do you feel, when you're with Tony? In control? That's not the way to love, Rachel. Love is stupid, unreasonable, idiotic, wonderful foolishness.'

His terrible logic was poisoning her mind. With all his astute and penetrating laser mind, he knew how she felt and was using it against her. It was so cruel!

Iván's wickedly skilful fingers had found the silken dip of her waist and was travelling around it with menacing confidence. Then the palm of his hand swept lovingly over the rounded swell of her stomach.

'You're not being very honest with yourself,' he murmured, heating her ear with mind-reeling little flurries of breath. 'Only I can give you what you are searching for. Why deny it?'

Oh, the voice was so seductive! The words were so true. Sweet agony ripped through her, laying her open to his assault.

'Please...' she moaned. 'I want to think...'

'No. You want to *feel*. Like this... and this...'

Rachel gasped as his tongue teased her mouth, telling her what he wanted, what he intended.

'Dammit, woman, you're driving me out of my mind! You want *me*,' said Iván savagely.

'I know,' she moaned, foolishly, sinking deep into the bed beneath his weight. His urgent, restless hands brought a bewildering need into her brain, as they slipped under her breasts and revelled in their weight, adoringly, delicately trailing in nerve-shattering paths over the passion-darkened buds that rose shamelessly to his mouth. He moistened them with his tongue as she stared at him, hypnotised, and then there was an indescribable sensation that totally destroyed her as he nursed at her breasts, one, then the other.

His mouth teased so she could feel its soft inner parts drawing smoothly with a terrible rhythm. In abandoned delight, she placed her hands on each side of his head and transferred him to the other breast and then back again, neither ever being satisfied as he tugged and suckled, sending impossibly sharp knives tearing through her body, opening it to him, reducing it to an inviting container, longing to be filled.

'Tell me you like this,' he muttered against her breast.

'I do!' she moaned.

'Angel, make me do what you want. Show me where to touch you,' he urged. 'Invite me!'

The desperate growl created fierce stabbing pains of desire. She was leaving. This would be the last time she would ever see him again. Fate owed her this one perfect and complete satisfaction of the urges which had been driving an unbidden ache of fierce heat in the core of her body.

'Yes. Yes, yes, *yes*!'

'I want you, I want you so much it hurts,' he said hoarsely.

'Kiss me hard, very hard,' she breathed. Crushing his whole weight on her, his mouth forced down on to hers, telling her, showing, demanding complete submission to his disturbing carnality. When he lifted his head, she could hardly breathe and her lips had swollen to the colour of cherries.

'Iván!' she said huskily.

'Now...where?' His voice was breaking up. It all but consumed her with its depths of longing.

'Everywhere,' she whispered. 'Oh, everywhere! The whole of my body needs you! You'll never satisfy me!'

'I will. Oh, Rachel, I will. Give me time.'

So he began his journey. The covers were ripped off, her nightdress slid impatiently from her body, and in a moment his shirt followed it to the floor. At the pressure of his naked chest, Rachel uttered little guttural sounds in her throat and Iván drew himself up on his hands, lightly brushing across her nipples, from side to side, with tantalising feathery touches from the dark hairs on his chest. Rachel's hands tore into his shoulders, gripping hard and bringing him down, scoring deep marks in his gloriously powerful back as they rolled over and over on the bed.

'Oh, you tiger,' he grinned as he lay beneath her, his eyes hot and sparkling. 'I am going to enjoy every perfect inch of you.'

She inhaled the man smell of him and gently licked each small twin peak of his chest, sending him crazy. With a quick flick, he had pinned her to the bed and was tasting the skin of her shoulder, sliding sinuously over her body as he did so.

'You're mine,' he muttered. 'Do you hear, Rachel?' He buried his face in her soft hair and breathed in its fragrance. He lifted her head for a moment, releasing her hair and drawing it either side of her head on to her breasts, till they were almost hidden. His hands smoothed down her hair rhythmically until Rachel thought she could never bear it if he continued, and could never bear it if he stopped. Wickedly, knowing this, he paused. In answer to his torture, she writhed like a cat beneath him and his black eyes closed in ecstasy.

'Such sweet torment!' he muttered. 'How long can I stand it? How much more do I have to restrain myself, to prove that your doe eyes, your slender nose, your crushed lips are mine? That this body was made for me and me alone? *Are* you ready?'

His fingers slid to worship the curve of her mouth, wondering at its beautiful lines. Slowly his lips lowered to take gentle possession and he closed his eyes in ecstasy, concentrating completely on that one perfect point on her body. He was sensational. With a moan, she stroked his blissful face with gentle fingers.

'I've never felt so powerful and so helpless,' he murmured against the softly trembling petals of her mouth.

Neither had she. Rachel wanted to tussle with him in a furious attempt to release some of the energy that threatened to shock both of them if she ever let it erupt. She wanted to tangle her arms and legs around him, roll over and over, kissing, eating, loving... She groaned, as his hands searched gently for the angle of her hipbone, and traced its ridge. He was using just his fingertips, knowing that to feel his touch, she would rise to meet him, thus co-operating in her own seduction. Rachel fought the urge to thrust into him, lying as tensed as a bow, waiting. And all she could hear was that wild pounding of her heart and Iván's soft, seductive voice, filling her head with madness.

'Oh, yes, you are ready,' he said thickly, his fingers the merest touch between her thighs. But they slid so easily that she knew the melting heat within her had begun its liquefaction in readiness for his lovemaking.

'Love me,' he breathed into her mouth, kissing her with tantalising sweetness. 'Please love me.'

Rachel's heart turned over at the intense yearning in his voice and the complete yielding of his once invulnerable personality. That was the factor she found so intensely erotic and appealing. She knew how he hid his inner feelings and guarded them jealously. This was his ultimate sacrifice to her.

'I need your love,' he muttered desperately.

'You have it,' she admitted with a groan. 'God help me, but I love you, Iván, as I've never loved anyone before. I love you so madly that I'm afraid.'

'It won't be long before you'll be too exhausted to be afraid,' he promised, his eyes tenderly passionate. 'Only I can satisfy you and only you can satisfy me. Our needs are identical. A need to give more love than most people dream about. We both have a bottomless well of it. There's only one way to begin plumbing the depths of that well, Rachel, and that's by expressing it like…this.'

A tender kiss brushed her brow. Rachel reached out for him as he lifted himself away, but she heard through her dazed and fuddled thoughts the sound of a belt being unlatched, the rasp of a zip, and the soft shuffling of material.

Iván's hand caressed her burning face. 'Tell me you love me again,' he said quietly. 'I need to hear it, over and over. I'm so uncertain of you, you see. I can hardly believe what you've just said. Tell me again. You're not going to marry Tony, are you? Swear that you don't love him. Not Tony, me. Me, Rachel … Love *me*.'

His brows were drawn into a deep frown. Power vibrated from him, as though he was willing her to confirm his words. When she hesitated, his eyes blazed fury, like a man whose plans were in deadly danger. She grew cold. Her skin chilled with numbing rapidity.

The truth dawned. He was still taking his revenge on his brother! She had fallen in love with a man who only wanted her body because, in conquering her, he triumphed over his despised brother, over his disinheritance. And now she knew that she wanted someone who loved her for herself alone. Nothing less would do. 'You can't do this to me!' she whispered in horror.

'Oh, I can,' he muttered.

Rachel saw his mouth closing in on her and she aimed a hard slap at his jaw, taking advantage of his shocked withdrawal to wriggle from beneath him and scramble from the bed, flattening herself against the wall like a trapped animal.

'What the... Rachel? What is it?'

'You unutterably despicable, evil-minded, loathsome...'

'Tell me what I've done,' he groaned. All the love she imagined she had seen had vanished. Only the hard, cynical Iván remained. The true Iván.

Rachel moaned at her stupidity. 'You're getting your own back on Tony, aren't you?' she breathed. 'All that talk of love was meaningless! You don't know what it is to love! You're cold through and through!'

He leapt up, grabbed her arms and shook her violently. 'No, Rachel, *no*!'

'Yes! In the morning, you were intending to flaunt the fact that yet again you'd seduced the woman he'd proposed to! Well, your Latin wiles haven't worked this time, Iván Posada!' she cried, her voice almost breaking in abject humiliation and misery. 'I won't give in to you, I won't! Not when you are so... *worthless!*'

Iván's teeth bared in a snarl, then her scornful eyes saw him struggle to compose himself and hide his evil feelings. 'You can't marry Tony,' said Iván in a voice devoid of all emotion. 'I won't let you!'

'Dog in the manger!' she yelled. 'He's all the things you aren't! I've been looking for someone like him,' she went on, wanting to hurt him and show she didn't care, that she wasn't breaking up inside. 'What business is it of yours what I do?'

'No! Without love in return, you'll be destroyed!'

'By him? What do you think *you've* done?'

Iván stared. Then he began to dress. Rachel cautiously reached for her dressing-gown and put it on, standing as far away from him as she could and wishing there was a door within reach for her to escape through.

'Sit down,' said Iván when he was dressed. 'Do I have to make you?' he yelled, shooting her a wild look, when she remained rigid and unmoving, locked in her icy, despairing world.

She sat on the edge of the bed while Iván paced up and down, expending his unreleased energy and passion in the fierce pounding. Then he stopped, gathered himself together with a supreme effort of will and faced her, his arms folded, his body leaning negligently against the wall.

'You're not being honest with yourself. You don't love him. I don't even think you desire him the way you desire me,' he said callously.

Rachel felt the wash of pink shame flood her body.

'You know I'm right. Surely you've more principles than to marry Tony to satisfy some ancient inheritance law? Supposing he meets a woman he really loves? What then? How would you feel? And how would you like to live the whole of your life without discovering what true love is?'

She stared aghast at his hard, uncompromising face. She *knew* what it was like, and it hurt. It hurt terribly.

'Rachel,' he said softly. 'For your own sake, don't get involved.'

'How can I trust anything you say?' she wailed. 'Tony and Emily and Mike swear you're a liar.'

'There's a good reason for that, Rachel. You see, whenever my mother appeared on the scene with me, my father visibly came alive. He was fond of Diana, but felt nothing of the wild, uncontrollable passion that he did for Teresa. And that upset everyone. His love for both of us shone nakedly in his eyes, and he'd hug me to him so hard that he all but bruised me. Think how that must have hurt Tony and Emily! They were more than willing to believe my grandparents' lies that my mother was evil and mercenary and that all I wanted was Latimer's.'

'Don't you?' she accused.

'I want my mother's name cleared,' he said tightly. 'And there's something else you ought to know. If the farm goes out of the family, both Emily and Mike will be left with nothing. No home, no income, no furniture, nothing. They have a vested interest in you. You could be their salvation. Now you understand why they were so keen when Tony raved about you as being the perfect, sweet and obedient potential little bride. Now do you see why they were so indecent in their haste to get you to the altar and why I've done everything I can to spare you this moment?'

'Everything?' she breathed.

'Yes. Everything.'

His black eyes held hers and it dawned on her that he really believed that his carefully arranged seduction of her was a kind act, designed to show her in the nicest possible way that she didn't love Tony and ought to withdraw from the scene. But it had been the cruellest thing that had ever happened to her in a lifetime of unkind and thoughtless actions. For he had torn her heart in two and she would never get it back together properly or make it whole again. The wound was too deep. For her, it was the end of any thoughts of love. The agony was too severe.

'Oh, you bastard,' she muttered miserably.

'Not such a bastard if I've saved you from a loveless marriage—and it would have been, wouldn't it?'

'I can't bear it,' she moaned, rocking herself backwards and forwards. 'I wish I'd never set eyes on any of you!'

For a long, shuddering moment, they both looked at each other, wishing back time to the day before they had met, willing Fate to reverse the clock and allow them the chance of avoiding each other and the mind-shattering emotions that were aroused every time they met.

'Half my life has been spent thinking "if only", Rachel,' he said sadly, tearing at her heart with his pain.

She wrung her hands, indecision marring her face. 'You have so much hatred in your heart.'

'I've been given so much.' He fixed her with his terrible eyes.

'And you hate Emily,' she said quietly.

'Wouldn't you, if you were me? She's turning Anna against me and is prepared to scheme and plot so that she can keep Anna and so Mike can continue to run the farm. To achieve those things, she's willing to let Tony go ahead with this hare-brained, selfish cruelty to you.'

'Will you leave?' she said despondently. 'I want to get some clothing on.'

'Do that while I make some coffee. We need to talk.'

With a listless shrug, she agreed. He'd want to discuss her severance pay. She couldn't stay now, after her embarrassing capitulation back there. He was an expert in dishing out humiliation. She loved him. He'd been her destiny, a terrible, disastrous destiny, but something she had to endure, nevertheless. Why did people have to fall in love and not have that love returned? Why had she been selected to suffer for the sake of two men's vengeance towards each other?

Her mind a mass of whirling thoughts, Rachel scrambled into some underwear and a warm orange shirt, pulling on a pair of red dungarees and rainbow socks. She needed a bit of colour to bolster her up.

'You look ready for a fight,' observed Iván when he saw her.

'I am,' she said grimly.

'Look,' he said, pushing a cup in front of her, 'what are you intending to do?' His tone was soft and sounded caring. Rachel's eyes blurred and she searched for her cup, spooning sugar into it briskly till she could see straight again.

'I'm leaving,' she said, steeling herself, 'immediately I've drunk this.'

'Have you considered Tony's reaction?' he asked. 'I think you ought to face the fact that Tony won't give you up. He can't afford the time. He's expended too much energy chasing you to waste it all. Finding and preparing another lamb for the slaughter could take a long time, and that's one thing he doesn't have. Everywhere you go, he'll pursue you.'

'No,' she protested.

'That's what he did with the last two.'

'What?' she said aghast, not even noticing how sweet her drink was.

'I had to work hard to discourage them,' said Iván sardonically.

'You're disgusting!'

Rachel was shocked at the fierce, tearing wave of jealousy this engendered. Her mouth had tightened in anger and she couldn't meet his eyes till she had gained some control of her fury.

'However,' he continued, amusement in his expression, 'there was only one way to stop him pestering them.'

'What?' she asked, rather frightened of the passions of the two men she had unwittingly aroused.

'They each got married.'

Not something she could achieve, she thought wryly.

'Oh, God! What am I going to do?' she muttered helplessly. 'Supposing I write him a letter, telling him firmly that I don't love him and wouldn't marry him if he was the last man on earth...'

'Try committing suicide,' muttered Iván. 'That's marginally more likely to stop him. And yet... I know what will.'

'For heaven's sake, what?' Rachel clutched at his shoulders desperately.

'Tell him you're marrying me,' he said quietly.

Rachel's eyes widened, and the pain in her heart slashed it so thoroughly that she flinched. The message was clear. He wanted the ultimate in revenge and this was an opportunity not to be missed. What a bastard he was! She dropped her lashes so that he didn't see her agonised longing. Marrying Iván had been her mindless dream—under different circumstances. Maybe a moon and a romantic dinner, she thought hysterically, not a threat from a man needing a wife so that he could keep possession of his home.

'Our engagement will give you time to get yourself together,' he suggested in his soft, velvet voice. 'Keep Tony off your back—I'm the only person he's afraid of. Do you know of any other man who'd do this?'

Oh, God! She wanted him! But like this... It was too ironic, too cruel. 'They'd retaliate by never letting you see Anna again. Would you risk losing her, for the sake of revenge?' she said coldly.

'Ah, revenge,' he said, his eyes kindling. Rachel thought of the way he made love and the primitive passion so near to the surface, and a tremor of desire ran through her. He wanted to satisfy his lust. 'I've been ordered off Latimer land as it is,' he reminded her. 'I shall have to fight to see my daughter again whether we pretend to be engaged or not. That's the offer. Take it or leave it. But your life will be hell if Tony pursues you.'

They wouldn't actually have to marry, just pretend to be engaged. She wouldn't have to sleep with Iván, or let him touch her. She dared not. If he did, she'd melt immediately. And for her own sanity, she must never give in to Iván. The desert he would leave behind when he had tired of her would be far worse than the longing she now cherished in her heart.

'All right,' she said shakily. 'I agree.'

Iván's whole body relaxed and she realised that every one of his muscles had been tensed. He really did want his moment of triumph over the Latimers badly!

'Rachel, I swear I will never touch you against your will, and I promised myself years ago that I would never marry again without love.'

'So you learned your lesson the first time! It's not much fun when you make a mistake, is it?'

'Not a lot.'

'Why did you marry your wife?'

'I wanted someone to love me,' he said huskily. 'I so desperately wanted to be loved.'

Sharp daggers scythed into Rachel's body. This man lived life with such mountainous highs and lows that it left her breathless. His passions and miseries reached far beyond those of any man she had known, and he was catching her up in them, dragging her along as an unwilling participant in his life.

'I think you've forfeited that right to love,' she said, cruelly wounding him in her anger. 'Tyrants are never liked, let alone loved.'

He winced. 'Pack your things. We'll go back to London now,' he said harshly.

CHAPTER EIGHT

THE hours passed slowly. Rachel had telephoned to tell Tony of her decision and that she would be living with Iván until the wedding. Tony didn't believe her. She listened to his tirade in horror, till Iván gently replaced the receiver. The phone rang again and he lifted it off the hook. For a moment, Rachel heard Tony's desperate pleas, faint and tragic, then Iván disconnected the line. She began to cry, in self-pity.

'I think we'd better get married quickly,' he said softly.

Rachel stiffened every sinew. Her soul had hungered for these very words that her mind was coldly rejecting.

'What on earth for?' she asked icily.

'Tony will hound you if you stay single. Emily and Mike will be pushing him. None of them want to lose Latimer's. Besides, I don't think they'd believe I'd accept a long engagement; I'm not the type. I'm hardly the kind of man to propose marriage and wait patiently for my wedding night. It would be like asking a starving man to wait a few hours for a casserole to be cooked: an unnecessary delay. Anyone really hungry would eat the food raw without waiting.'

'You hardly fit into the category of starving men,' said Rachel sarcastically.

'Oh, I'm starving,' he said, pausing for a moment and fixing her with his laser stare. 'Not in the way you mean, though.'

She was starving, thought Rachel savagely. She knew she didn't want to leave Iván. Being with him in any way was better than not being with him at all. He had snared her with his black magic. She was totally lost. He was using that fatal need she had for him and was exerting pressure on her in every way he knew how. He did that with everyone; he found their flaws, their secrets, and used that knowledge against them without mercy.

'There isn't anything else for it, is there?' he said expressionlessly.

'I don't know what you mean,' she said huffily and marched out, hurrying to the kitchen for safety and starting to poach herself some eggs for a late breakfast.

'Two eggs for me,' called Iván, collecting the morning papers from the hall.

In deliberate defiance, she continued with her own breakfast, ignoring his order.

He slapped the newspapers on the table as usual. 'Aren't you having any breakfast?' he asked, inspecting the eggs.

'*You* aren't unless you do your own. Those are mine,' she said calmly.

'Stubborn child,' he chided gently, ruffling her mane of hair.

'Don't *do* that!' she yelled.

'How wild you're getting, Rachel,' he smiled. 'I'm not sure Tony would see that as being suitable.'

'Forget Tony!'

'I wish I could. It's all very well,' he said, laying bacon into a pan, 'but you have to decide what you're doing.'

'Oh, move out of the way!' She took the spatula from him and added a little oil to the pan.

'Thanks,' he grinned. 'I need looking after.'

'You need looking after like a piranha needs teeth,' she snapped.

'Every woman I meet wants to mother me,' he said innocently. 'Cook things and so on.'

'Rubbish! You promise unmitigated, unrelenting nights of sex, and that excites them. After, they probably feel the least they can do is stoke up your energies again.'

'No, really. They like my total lack of softness. They like me being so masculine. It makes them feel very...' his voice took on a seductive quality '...female.'

'What arrant nonsense! Total masculinity implies a lack of empathy with women. You're out of touch. That's not what we like nowadays.'

'You could have fooled me,' said Iván softly, placing his hands around her waist and running them upwards.

'Either you want your breakfast on a plate, or you want it, frying pan and all, down the front of your trousers. You decide,' said Rachel gripping the handle of the pan tightly.

He gave a low laugh and moved away, allowing Rachel to relax her tensed muscles. Even breakfast was a major drama with this man! With her mouth set tightly, she tipped his bacon and eggs on to a plate and served up her own breakfast.

'It would be safer if you married me,' he said gently.

'Safe?' she scorned. 'No wife of yours would be safe from anything!'

His eyes narrowed dangerously. 'If you decide to go it alone,' he said in a sinister voice, 'I'll keep after you myself. I don't like having my passions aroused and not satisfied. One day I'll get you somewhere alone and touch you and all hell will be let loose.'

True. Now he was forcing her to add lying to her shame. 'I'd never give in to you! I can't bear men who think of nothing but their animal lusts! Not everyone needs sex ten times a night like you,' she said angrily.

'Ten times?' He smiled silkily. 'Is that what you're longing for? No woman has been able to excite me to such excesses yet, Rachel. Maybe you could be the first.'

He was moistening his mouth with the tip of his tongue, as if in preparation for her. Rachel wanted to sweep everything off the table and scramble over it to sit in his lap, tear open his shirt and kiss him wildly. Instead, she took her uneaten breakfast to the sink and tipped it into the waste disposal unit, listening with satisfaction as the steel blades pulverised it. Her own violence was beginning to frighten her. If she wasn't careful, she'd do something she'd really regret.

'That is,' he added harshly, 'if Tony doesn't reach you before I do.'

'What? You don't think . . .' She stared at him aghast, and ran a weary hand over her forehead.

'You need to know what you're letting yourself in for,' he said quietly. 'I can protect you from him if we're married.'

'I could go far away.'

'Never far enough, either from him or me,' said Iván in a dangerous tone. 'I'd follow you to the ends of the earth. You'll never escape. I intend to have you. From the time I discovered I had nothing of my father to remember him by, nothing from his family but hate, I've always got everything else I wanted. Always. And I want you, Rachel. Ever since you trotted into my study in that ridiculous grey suit with your waif-and-stray face and woman's body. Ever since you made me burn with hellfires when you had flu and aroused me, and I walked away like a noble idiot. I'm never going to let you go, so work out your future from that promise.'

'What is your main motive for marriage?' she asked in a low voice. He had made every nerve in her body vibrate with each word he uttered, and she couldn't take much more.

Iván pushed aside his emptied plate and leaned his arms on the table. 'The reasons, my sweet, are many and complex. Certainly, it stops Tony doing something I consider despicable. I won't have him hurting you and treating you as a convenience.'

'But *you* can! And it'll mean that he loses the farm. Will that please you?'

'No!' he snarled. 'God in heaven, what do you take me for? However much I dislike Tony, he is my half-brother and I'd rather he owned Latimer's than a stranger. But surely you must understand that I abhor the idea of anyone marrying without deep and long-lasting love! Think what it did to my father, and how it soured the rest of the family!'

'But you . . .' He was intending to marry without love, but of course *he* could break all the rules he made!

'Tony wouldn't be happy, seeing your disappointed face every morning. You need to love, Rachel, to care deeply, to experience great passion!'

She winced. 'What of your own obsession to have me?' she asked.

'I wish to God I didn't feel so violently about you. Obsession makes no one happy,' he said quietly. 'It causes terrible anguish. Only by coming to terms with their potential and limitations can anyone begin to handle inner rage and resentment. Believe me, I'm an expert in obsession and inner rage.'

'Yes. It shows.'

'Only because it suits me to let it be seen,' he countered tightly.

'And Anna? You'll lose the right to see her, perhaps. Emily could do that to hurt you.'

'Not if I'm married,' he said. 'I could gain custody by marrying.'

Quickly, to hide her shock, she rose and pushed her plate into the dishwasher, pretending to rearrange some of the crockery. So that was it. In marrying her, he gained a bedmate and his daughter. Somewhere, in the back of her mind, Rachel knew that she'd harboured the thought that he might come to love her, and that their closeness in the past was more than her imagination. Now, any romantic notions had been completely swept away. He was using her as cruelly as Tony had intended. The only difference was that she loved Iván and would be more deeply hurt by marriage to him. But she couldn't say no, even then.

'Rachel, I know that I'm asking a lot of you, to take on my child. But I'm very disturbed at the way Emily is poisoning the child's mind against me. You heard the way she speaks to the kiddie. I'm not imagining it, am I?'

'No, Iván. I wouldn't be certain that she intends the result she gets, but Anna is definitely confused.'

'Oh, Emily knows exactly what she's doing,' said Iván bitterly. 'I don't even like the way she's turning Anna into a prototype little girl, all ribbons and bows and silent sweetness. I see a spunky little girl under her reserve, but she's too crushed to let it out very often. Sometimes when she's with me, I can't hold her back, she's so irrepressibly exuberant.'

'She's got your vitality,' said Rachel. 'Your drive and assertiveness. It's at odds with Emily's teaching.'

'Emily's teaching includes ensuring that Anna hates me. She's using my child as a weapon, and I can't stand it much longer.'

Rachel flinched at the despair in his voice. 'You're both pulling her heartstrings. Anna doesn't know what to do. I think you either have to abandon Anna altogether, or take care of her yourself.'

'I know.'

'What of Emily's feelings? She's mothered your daughter for years!'

'I can't deny that she loves Anna, but so do I and I've been denied my child through no fault of my own. She's mine! Emily is young; she can adopt other children, children she can really call her own.'

Rachel was too bound up in how all this affected her to query Iván's part in Anna being fostered. 'What's the difference between my sacrifice for Tony and my sacrifice for you?' asked Rachel angrily. Both men were as selfish as each other!

'Silly girl! I can offer you more than he can,' smiled Iván.

The centre of Rachel's throat constricted at the thought of what he could offer, and her eyes flickered with an involuntary reaction to his sensual mouth, travelling down over the husky male shoulders, his spreading chest, the firm biceps...

'You said you'd never force me!'

'I won't,' he said, amused.

'And that you'd never marry again without love!' Acknowledge that, her heart begged. Then tell me you care, that you really adore me, that every breath I take is precious, that you long to possess me, body and soul.

'That's true,' he said without expression. 'I didn't say it had to be both of us, did I?'

He'd rumbled her. He knew. Those foolish words of love that had escaped from her idiotically big mouth had come back to haunt her. Why did she let herself be for ever at his mercy because of an unguarded tongue? She poured herself some more coffee with a trembling hand.

'You knew all along I'd have to marry you, that Tony wouldn't relent, didn't you?' she said tonelessly.

'Yes. I didn't dare tell you at the time because you'd just take off into the blue and I wouldn't be around to protect you when Tony came on strong with the sob stuff.

What's the hesitation, Rachel? You know you want to marry me,' he said, irritatingly frank as usual.

'I don't think I could stand your infidelity,' she said in a whisper.

'No problem,' he grinned airily.

'Oh yes, there is! You couldn't be faithful if your life depended on it.'

'I would be, to you.'

'Huh! Mr Try-them-all Posada?' she taunted.

He laughed in delight, his face breaking into the most annoyingly wonderful grin as his teeth flashed whitely at her and crushed any resistance. He really oughtn't to be so wickedly devastating! She wanted him in her bed, to wake up beside him, to see his face unguarded, soft and gentle.

'I'm not a rake,' he said quietly. 'I prefer long, slow and tantalising build-ups before bedding a woman.' His fingers stroked her hand which gripped the handle of her cup in manic fear.

'Let go,' she snapped, suppressing the twirling coils of desire. 'I want to drink my coffee.'

'Liar,' he grinned. 'You want me to make mad passionate love to you.'

'You don't honestly expect me to believe that you'll be faithful, do you?' she snapped, ignoring his flippant remark.

'Marriage seems to have that effect on me,' he admitted. 'I was before, I can be again. If I have a woman at home, waiting for me, why should I trouble to venture elsewhere?'

'Variety,' she said scathingly.

'Oh, we'll have variety,' he said with a sexy grin that made Rachel's heart flip over. 'I'm renowned for it. You don't have to question the quality of our sex life, do you?'

'What is the strongest reason for marrying me?' she asked in a small voice.

Iván scanned her face, taking in the anxiety, the pain and the sorrow. 'You'll find out,' he promised. 'Stop trying to fight. We both have very strong reasons for marrying each other. I think we'll be pleasantly surprised at the result.'

'If you don't get custody, will you divorce me? I have to know,' she asked wildly, her eyes huge and troubled.

Iván reached out and held her shaking hand. 'I will never leave you,' he said.

'Did you tell your first wife that?' she cried, biting her lip. Promises could be easily made and easily broken.

'No. You don't know much about me, do you? Listen. For twenty-five years I thought that I would inherit Latimer's. When I heard that my grandfather hadn't even mentioned me in his will, I was nearly out of my mind with the waste of all those years of hope. I was nameless and my mother branded a whore. There was no one to comfort me. I met Caroline soon after and she tried to lift me out of my black patch. I married her, thinking love would grow between us because I wanted it so much.'

'And yet you abandoned her, even though she'd cared for you.'

'I did *what*?'

He looked so blazingly angry that Rachel was nervous. 'Tony said . . .'

A hiss of breath escaped Iván's lips. 'He's a liar! I swear it, on my mother's name. Caroline and I had both decided I should go to the States to look for work, so we could start afresh in a new country. She wasn't home when I rang to tell her about the job I'd landed. Eventually I discovered she was at the farm, but Tony wouldn't let me speak to her.'

'She was pregnant!' accused Rachel.

'I didn't *know*,' said Iván in a pained voice. 'I swear I didn't. I wrote, I telephoned, but I couldn't fly back for some time, because of my contract—I'd expected her to join me, you see. By the time I did get to England, it was too late. Caroline was ensconced with Tony and Emily, and they had smashed my marriage with lies. Even then, she didn't tell me that she was pregnant, presumably because she was so angry. She wouldn't believe I hadn't gone off the rails and slept with half a dozen women a night. She knew how greedy I was,' he said with a grim smile. 'She couldn't accept that I have enough will-power to deny myself immediate gratification.'

'What happened?'

'Tony threatened to set the police on me and swear I'd been molesting Caroline in some bestial fashion. God! It's a wonder I haven't swung for his murder! Now do you see why I hate him?' he grated. 'He ruined my marriage and denied me knowledge of my child. Caroline had a riding accident and died asking Emily to care for Anna. The first I knew I was a father was at Caroline's funeral. Imagine the shock,' he whispered. 'Just imagine.'

Rachel wanted to draw his tortured face to her breast and hold him till all the pain had gone. He'd been through hell and she hadn't known. She could flatten Tony herself for what he'd done to Iván. 'It's—it's terrible. Tragic. But . . . why didn't you fight for Anna?'

'Christ! Do you think I didn't?' he raged. 'I nearly went bankrupt trying to get custody of my own kid! You see, Emily had kept every snippet of lying gossip about me. Any female within a hundred yards of me was liable to be pounced on by reporters and photographers and quizzed. Twice, the perfectly respectable wives of my mates at work were pestered during a dinner given by the magazine's management. I stood their filthy insinuations for just so long, and then laid them out cold.'

'I saw the article about that,' said Rachel. 'I must say, I thought you sounded a drunken lecher.'

'Exactly,' he growled. 'So did the rest of the world, so did the courts. I was deemed unsuitable to care for a small child. Besides, Anna didn't know me; all she had heard was that a nasty dark man was trying to take her away—oh, you've no idea what lies that kiddie has been told! I admit my stupidity. I admit my mistakes. I can't live my life over again! What I did has come back to torment me! *If*, I think, *if* I hadn't tried to make a new life... *If* my mother hadn't fallen in love with the son of her employer... *If* Emily didn't hate and fear me... *If, if, if!*'

CHAPTER NINE

RACHEL stared at Iván's hands, gripping hers in a desperate clasp. They were quite still and it seemed that the world stood still for a moment, too, waiting for her response.

'I'll marry you,' she said quietly.

And then he did an extraordinary thing. He lifted her two hands to his lips and kissed each palm in turn. Rachel's heart flipped. She was his slave. Unwilling, yes, but his slave, nevertheless. He would make love to her and they would both enjoy it, but his heart would be always closed, whereas hers was terrifyingly vulnerable to meaningless gestures... like hand-kissing.

'What—what do we do now?' she breathed, her lashes fluttering like panic-stricken butterflies.

'Don't tempt me,' he muttered, releasing her hands abruptly. 'It depends on whether you want to be married in up-market Chelsea, in which case one of us will have to establish residence for three weeks somewhere around the King's Road, or whether you can put up with the Register Office in Marylebone Road and we get a common licence. That means one day's wait.' His eyes gleamed. 'As far as I'm concerned, the quicker the better.'

Rachel experienced an upsurge of panic. It threatened to lend power to her legs and convey her right out of Iván's life and into anonymity.

'The less time we have to consider our actions, the better,' he suggested. 'And I can begin to file for custody.'

'Oh. Yes, of course.' The ultimate in put-downs.

'And I can get you legally into bed,' he threatened.

'Chelsea,' she said breathlessly.

'Wrong. Marylebone.'

'You said I could choose!'

'I didn't say I'd accept your decision,' he said sardonically. 'It doesn't suit me. Come on, we'll go now.'

'I won't be pushed around by you!' cried Rachel, trying to establish at least some kind of rights of her own. Iván would completely dominate her if she wasn't careful.

His hand snaked out, relentlessly dragging her towards him, till she was trapped between his knees. There was a glazed look about his eyes and Rachel knew he was about to test her resistance. She didn't want that, didn't want the humiliation when he proved she would crawl adoringly at his feet for the pleasure of his touch, just like all his other women.

'I hate you, Iván Posada! I hate your autocratic, domineering manner! Don't push me too far!'

'How far is that?' he murmured, sliding a hand to her thigh.

'We'd better go, if we're to get this licence,' she said hastily.

Iván grinned. 'How dare you spoil my persuasion! I was looking forward to it.'

'Well, I wasn't,' she said crisply.

With a mocking laugh, he stood up, his thighs warm against hers, chuckling evilly as she fled into her bedroom for a warm sweater.

'By the way,' he said, when they emerged from the Register Office. 'There's one thing I can't give you: a honeymoon. Not till later. I'll have to fix it up with the rag I work for. And there's Anna's birthday—I'll want to be there.'

'Mike said . . .'

'To hell with what he said! I'm getting a temporary injunction, on the grounds that my situation has changed. Soon I'll be a respectable married man. Well, married,' he said with a rueful smile. 'I hope to God I never become respectable. You wouldn't like me half as much.'

'Will you bring Anna back here for her birthday treat?' It worried her that he hadn't warned his daughter. What would she think? It might make her unsure of Iván's love.

'No, I thought we'd pick her up at Diana's and take her off somewhere like the Dolphinarium or the Toy Museum. There's lots of things we can do with her around Brighton, and we've got a little while to decide what. Our first priority, though, is finding somewhere to live.'

'Why not the apartment?' she asked, as they reached the car.

'I'll drive.' His dark brows met in a thick dark line. 'London is no place to bring up a child. Or children.'

'You ... you want us to have children?' The thought had never crossed her mind, she'd been so taken up with everything else!

'Don't you?' The jet eyes were remote.

Rachel shuddered. What wild children might she mother? 'I—I want children,' she faltered.

'Good. Because I will be filling you with the opportunity to create them as soon as we're married.'

Sadness filled her. This was everything she had dreamed of, but the reality was flawed.

'I thought we'd find somewhere on the London-Victoria line, near to the station. We'll look at the map when we get back.'

'Perhaps you'd drop me in Oxford Street,' she ventured. 'I need some new clothes.'

His brows lifted. 'Sexy underwear?'

'No!'

'Yes. And we'll go to Bond Street. To hell with the department stores. My wife wears silk or satin next to her skin.'

'Please, no, Iván! I don't know how to handle myself in those places. They'll look down on me...'

'My darling, what they think is unimportant. And if anyone looks like snubbing you, they'll get a tongue-lashing they'll never forget, believe me.'

He parked on a double yellow line. Knowing Iván, she thought with a sigh, as she trailed humbly behind his elegant figure into a new world of couture, he wouldn't get a parking ticket and the Bentley wouldn't get clamped. That was the kind of justice on this earth.

They spent a wonderful day on an extravagant spending spree. When Rachel discovered just how generous Iván intended to be, and how much pleasure it gave him to see her sparkling eyes as she stroked the beautiful materials, she allowed him to persuade her to go mad. She bought clothes so ego-boosting that when they stopped for lunch she was on Cloud Nine.

Iván ushered her into a small Italian restaurant and sat back in the plush seat, eyeing the changed woman. A little bit of spoiling, the pleasure of sensual material, well cut, flattering clothes, and a single red rose, had wrought a startling change. She oozed a radiant self-confidence that affected everyone around her. Several times Iván had been forced to glare at other men admiring the long-maned beauty at his side. And, more satisfying, many women had given Rachel envious glances. Not—as they usually did—because of him, but because they resented and were jealous of her fresh, innocent beauty, flooded with happiness. For she was pretending that they were both in love and, however foolish that was, it made her unutterably happy.

'Isn't this heavenly?' cried Rachel, her eyes agog. She made a mental note that she'd learn how to cook Italian food. It seemed to be his favourite.

'Bloody pretentious,' grumbled Iván. 'But they do the best *salsa verde* in London.'

'Oh.' She subsided, crushed.

Iván reached out and caught her hand. 'Sorry,' he muttered. 'A touch of the vitriol. It's become a habit. You like this place, I like this place.'

'Is this the ''New Improved Washed Whiter'' Iván Posada?' she enquired.

He fingered his tanned face wryly. 'Miracles take a little longer.'

'What are we doing after lunch?' she asked, spooning up her *passatelli*.

'More shopping. Then back for a cup of tea, argue over the map and where we're going to live, then dinner and a show.'

'You don't have to do all this, you know,' said Rachel earnestly. 'This is a convenient arrangement for both of us—I don't need entertaining.'

'It passes the time.'

Rachel sighed at the snapped words. It did, indeed! She was quieter over the *saltimbocca* and stuffed peaches, thinking about their future together. Iván would quite probably be gentlemanly towards her some of the time, ignore her often, yell at her a lot and slake his lust frequently. It would be an interesting marriage. Would he ever really trust her?

After lunch, they wandered to Tiffany's. He asked if she would remove her wedding ring, and as she did so the whole reality of what she was doing came home to her very strongly. She was tying herself up for what might be a lifetime to this difficult man, who refused to let anyone into his heart, who would not drop that guard of his and share himself. Rachel worried that her love wouldn't be able to stand the problems ahead.

'Sapphires or emeralds?' he asked, as they went in.

'I don't know,' she answered in a daze.

'If I tell you the best emeralds come from Colombia...'

'Emerald, then,' she smiled.

The ring she chose was beautiful. As Iván slipped it on her finger and gave her a delicate kiss on her lips, her heart thudded with secret happiness.

'Emeralds stand for love,' said Iván. 'Very appropriate.'

She frowned. He didn't have to mock her. To her surprise, he didn't buy a wedding ring. They returned to the apartment and warned Daniel that he would be receiving an avalanche of parcels the next day. Iván took her to see *Phantom of the Opera* and held her hand all the way through. When they arrived home again, she declined the offer of a nightcap, feeling overwhelmingly tired.

'It's been a wonderful day, thank you,' she said to Iván.

'My pleasure,' came his deep voice. 'Tomorrow we'll drive down to Lewes and have a look around, shall we?'

That was where they hoped to set up home. Rachel nodded happily and a yawn escaped from her gentle mouth.

'Before you go to bed, I'd like to ask you something. No strings attached.' Iván shifted awkwardly.

She was suddenly alert. What now?

'This ring was given to me by my mother before she left England. It's not much, only a cheap little thing. But it is gold and she wanted me to give it to my wife. I wonder if you would wear it when we're married.'

She looked down at the plain narrow band in his palm. Touched by the gesture, Rachel felt a warmth towards him. 'Of course. Was it Caroline's?'

He frowned. 'No. She wanted something more valuable.'

Tears formed in Rachel's eyes. 'It would be valuable to me,' she managed, and swung blindly into her room.

There were times when there was an advantage in being arrogant and as subtle as a pile-driver, mused Rachel, as Iván drove her back to London through the late evening traffic the next day.

Enchanted with a house near Lewes station, she had begged him with her eyes to like it, too. It was big and rambling, with a confusing number of rooms, doors in odd places and creaking, spiral oak staircases. Rachel loved the nooks and crannies and the fact that it wasn't intimidatingly regal. Iván had explored the brick-paved cellar with interest, and she knew he was mentally planning where he would rack his wine. She had already laid out preserves on the stone-slab ledges! In the garden, with its high old flint walls, were quince, plum and pear trees, and one huge Bramley which was dropping big rosy apples on to the lawn.

Iván glanced over indulgently at the dreamy-faced woman beside him in the car. 'Which bedroom for Anna?' he asked.

'Oh, the one with the powder-room! She'll love that,' enthused Rachel, flicking back her hair.

'So long as she doesn't want an eighteenth-century wig to hang on the powdering pegs,' grinned Iván.

Rachel smiled happily. He had been as fascinated as she at the tiny closet. 'We must ask about that nursery school, and go and see the local primary head, too,' she planned. 'Then...'

'Wait. Let's get married first, shall we? And our offer hasn't definitely been accepted.'

'It's ours, I know it is. You had the estate agent and the owner in such a flat spin, offering the asking price and temporary accommodation...'

'I want that house,' he said quietly.

'I'm so glad,' she said, her eyes betraying her joy.

Iván's hand briefly covered hers in an understanding gesture and Rachel felt the emotions of the last few days endangering her composure.

'Oh, darn!' she mumbled, trying to find a handkerchief.

Iván frowned. 'Don't cry, Rachel. I can't handle women's tears. Stop it! Stop it, for God's sake!'

When she continued to sniff, his hand strayed to the back of her neck. She stiffened, pulling away with an involuntary movement.

'Does my touch upset you so much?' he asked harshly.

'Yes, it does,' she said with feeling. 'Iván, I'm not sure...'

'Christ!' He swerved, narrowly missing a taxi and earning a torrent of abuse from the driver. 'You can't back out now. I told Anna on the telephone, and she's like a smug cat with her secret.'

'You *told* her? Without consulting me? That was unfair!'

'She had to know,' he snapped. 'If she'd been upset...'

'You would have kicked me out and found someone she would accept,' said Rachel bitterly, all her hackles raised. It wasn't very pleasant, knowing you were marrying someone to be a kind of Good Conduct medal, in order to impress the courts with your air of homely domesticity.

'Don't be silly,' he coaxed, squeezing her knee.

Rachel thrust his hand away. 'Don't!' she bit out sharply.

She felt him draw away from her mentally, the cold mask lacquering his features into immobility. They drove in silence, with Rachel licking her wounds. Her head had become one huge adventure playground, it seemed, thoughts and desires helter-skelter, see-sawing, swinging, sliding. For the rest of the journey, she talked to herself over and over again, repeating coldly, 'He does not love me, he will not love me, sometimes he doesn't even like me.' She must not give him any ammunition. One day he'd use her weaknesses, her trust, to hurt her so deeply she'd never recover.

After an evening when Rachel had worked with icy calm and a cool, offhand attitude to make her position clear and convince him that she was indifferent to his charms, they had said goodnight more like polite acquaintances than two people who were going to be married the next day.

If anything else had failed to cool her romantic nature, the wedding ceremony would have done so very successfully.

Iván had spent some time in the morning on the telephone, handling a difficult conversation with Emily. He had obtained an injunction, preventing her from denying him access to Anna. Rachel knew from the drained hollows of his face as Emily spoke that some unpleasant things were being said. It didn't put him in a very good mood, to say the least.

When the conversation ended, he replaced the receiver very quietly and shut himself in the study. Rachel changed out of her casual jeans and sweater nervously, wondering whether she ought to remind him they were getting married in half an hour's time.

She was all fingers and thumbs, pulling on the luxur- ious little froths of French underwear that made her feel so wicked, and it was a relief to hide her suddenly sexy- looking body with the new soft wool dress. It was in a wonderful buttercup-yellow, and totally altered her ap- pearance, draping and clinging to make the most of her good points and minimise her faults.

Carefully, she applied a little make-up to cover her pallor and smoothed a little bronze eye-shadow over her lids to bring out the lights in her eyes. Then, a magazine open at the appropriate page, she followed the instruc- tions till her hair had been scooped up on top of her head in a loose and flattering style. It seemed to make her eyes look enormous. She was almost pretty.

Her watch told her that they ought to be leaving. Her trembling fingers fumbled with hatpins and secured a tiny yellow pillbox hat on the back of her head. Bronze shortie gloves, handbag and shoes with ridiculous stil- etto heels were added to the ensemble and checked sev- erely in the mirror, then the matching yellow coat with mandarin collar was dropped over her arm and she was ready.

Iván rose from the living-room couch as she came out of the bedroom, his only response a brief nod of ap- proval. Rachel's heart plummeted and a sick feeling filled her stomach. This wasn't the wedding day she'd looked forward to.

'Let's go,' he said, tension tightening his face muscles.

He looked stunning. The new charcoal-grey suit curved so beautifully on his body that Rachel longed to throw her arms around him and claim him for her own. The long slide of his leg on the seat next to her sent shivers down her back; the immaculate knife-creases in the trousers disturbed only by the muscular spread of his thighs. Her glance slid sideways. A darkly tanned hand lay negligently on the seat. She examined minutely the neatly cut fingernails, the long, sensitive fingers that could touch with such exquisite delicacy.

They had taken a taxi. It dropped them outside the Register Office and Iván's hand guided her elbow—just as well, because everything from then on became a blur. She wasn't really there, this was no real marriage.

Iván was so tense, so wound up, hostility exuding from every pore. They were standing before the Registrar now. He might back out. The very thought made her feel sick, and she flung a nervous glance at him, hating his hunted look.

She knew he'd almost run, pell-mell, that only his savage will-power had forced him to remember why he was doing this. At that moment she hated him, the hate mixing with the love and the longing to produce utter despair. She would do her part. She would create a home environment for Anna to be happy in. But she would never allow him to touch her. That part was dead.

The whole procedure ground on bleakly. They emerged, politely thanked the two passers-by who had acted as witnesses, and took a taxi home.

Iván had tried to put an arm around her in the taxi, but she had shaken him off, knowing that she'd burst into tears if he tried to assert his conjugal rights.

'Rachel——'

'No, don't touch me. I can't bear the idea of you touching me!' she grated.

'But...' His pained breath rasped in her face.

'Get away!' she screamed.

The taxi driver swore and jerked his head around. 'You OK, miss? You want me to throw him out?'

Miss! God help her, she was married now to a sex maniac. Rachel groaned. 'No, it's all right. Please drive on. I'll tell you when to stop.'

'What the hell are you doing?' growled Iván.

She didn't answer. She watched the people thronging the streets, wondering what would happen when they got back to the apartment, how long it would be before the seduction began. Iván was about to get everything he wanted. Her teeth caught at her lower lip savagely. What a fool she was! She'd thought marriage was all she wanted, that her love would supply the romance and the love. Well, Mrs Posada, she told herself bitterly, that wasn't enough.

She wanted to be wooed, courted, cherished, spoken to in loving tones.

'What had you planned to do this afternoon?' she asked in remote tones.

'What? Rachel, we've just got married! What do you think I'd planned!'

As she thought. 'Driver, would you stop here for a moment, please?'

Iván watched her, chewing his lips angrily as she slipped from the taxi and bought five magazines from a bookstall.

'What are you trying to prove?' he asked, as they drove on and she developed a sudden deep interest in couture fashion pages.

'Absolutely nothing,' she said in calm surprise, arching one eyebrow at him. She would not be hurt by him, she would not! She would not care that he wore no wedding ring to announce that he was now a married man and strictly off limits. She wouldn't care that he hadn't cuddled her and soothed her nerves before the wedding, or that he had no inclination to do so now. They arrived at King's Reach and she swept in ahead of him, bestowing a brilliant smile on the blue-eyed Daniel.

Before Iván could make any pretence of a marriage ritual by carrying her over the threshold, she had opened

the door with her own key and stalked in, discarding
bag, coat, hat and shoes as she went. He came up behind
her and she moved away quickly, seeing that his hands
had been raised to take her by the shoulders.

'Rachel——' he began helplessly.

'Would you mind getting me a drink?' she asked.

'In the middle of the afternoon?'

'Yes.'

His shoulders squared and the cold mask wiped his
face of emotion. Only the glittering eyes betrayed his
feelings.

'Here.'

'Lovely.' She took a sip and then another, and walked
away, busying herself by hanging up her coat in her
wardrobe, conscious that he'd followed and his eyes
watched every movement she made.

'What are you doing?' he asked quietly.

'Putting my coat away.'

'That is no longer your bedroom,' he pointed out.

'You mean we're sharing?'

'God!'

She was so much in control of herself, hiding so well
behind the shell she had created, that she was almost
proud of her self-possession. With an unconsciously elegant movement, she sat in a comfortable chair and
opened a magazine. 'Would you like me to get some
dinner this evening or shall we go out?' she asked
casually.

'That can be decided later,' he said with equal control.

Rachel stared uncomprehendingly at the glossy magazine, hoping she was correctly timing the speed at which
she turned the pages. Sounds told her that Iván had
pulled his tie loose, removed his jacket and was unbut-
toning his shirt.

Suddenly, the magazine was snatched from her grasp
and flung across the room.

Iván stood over her, his dark eyes blazing with a cold anger, his mouth that unnerving granite-hard line.

'I was reading that,' she complained sharply, meeting his eyes fearlessly.

'No, you weren't.'

Rachel found her body melting inside with the intensity of his raking gaze as it ran over every inch, lingering in calculating ownership on her breasts and hips. Hating his lack of sensitivity, she averted her gaze and stared haughtily out of the window.

'Look all you like,' she said distantly. 'But if you try to force yourself on me I shall fight you tooth and nail.'

'Why are you doing this to me?' he breathed.

Because you don't love me, she moaned silently. It's no good unless you do. I can't just have sex with you, that isn't enough. I must be in love and think I am loved. She shivered.

'I'm not in the mood. I'm suddenly rather tired of being manipulated. All my life I've obediently fallen in with everything that was asked of me. "You can't stay with the Lakers any longer, Rachel, they're having a baby of their own." "You must leave the Fielding family, Rachel, their son is at a dangerous age." "Marry me, I want your body." "Work for me, I need a driver." "Divorce me, I love someone else." It goes on and on, Iván! I thought I was taking control of my life, but I'm not! All I've done is to satisfy you!'

'Not yet, you haven't.'

'No, and I have absolutely no wish to do so, either.'

'You don't mean that,' he coaxed.

'Like hell I don't!' she yelled. 'Touch me and I'll hit you!'

Iván grew still, his face expressionless. With a slight nod of his head, he turned and strode into his study.

CHAPTER TEN

Long, terrible days followed, and even worse interminable nights. Iván avoided all physical contact with her now he had his token wife to display for the court's benefit. They slept apart—even virtually lived apart, since he apparently found it irritating to be in the same room for very long. He employed a new chauffeur from an agency, putting up with the fact that the man was hardly on instant call, since he lived some way out of the centre of London. But that, it seemed, he found preferable to spending time in her company.

Rachel felt increasingly isolated from human society, cooped up in the flat for most of the day. She had expected a small measure of relief in the occasional days with Anna, but Iván had been plunged unexpectedly into a frenzy of work that forced him to break two arranged meetings.

Unhappy and bored, Rachel prowled around the apartment, wondering what would happen if she just took off and disappeared. Only the thought of having Tony on her tail prevented her from doing so. And somewhere in the back of her mind was the forlorn hope that, once Anna came to live with them, she could at least be a good stepmother and her relationship with Iván might mellow.

If the weather had been kinder, she would have spent more time walking around London's parks and embankments. As it was, the wind and rain were so atrocious that on most days she was reduced to watching

day-time television, or listening to the radio, hardly able
to raise the energy to prepare a meal for herself.

The boredom was driving her mad! Iván came home
late, having eaten a meal already. Either he watched television in silence or he retired to the bedroom and put
on the stereo, playing violent music that poured through
the apartment in a frenzy of tormented sound.

One morning, as usual, she politely presented her
cheek for his farewell kiss—the 'appearance's sake kiss'
she called it—and stayed by the door, absently staring
after Iván's departing figure.

'Wishing the hours would race by, Mrs Posada?'
smiled Daniel, from across the foyer.

She sighed. 'Wishing I had something to do today,'
she admitted, stupidly pleased that someone had spoken
to her. 'Morning, Jarvis.'

Daniel came over as Jarvis, the relief doorman, took
his place. 'Tried the Museum of London? Clockmakers'
Exhibition? Diamond Centre?' She had nodded list-
lessly at each one.

'I need a job. Part-time, casual work. I don't know
how long we'll be here,' she said.

'I might be able to help you there.' He grinned. 'I
have a wide range of contacts. Female.'

'I bet you have,' she laughed. It was a long time since
she'd laughed so easily.

'What sort of thing are you looking for?'

Rachel hesitated. Boredom won over wisdom. 'Why
don't you come in and I can tell you over a cup of
coffee?' she suggested.

Daniel's eyes kindled. 'I'd like that, Mrs Posada.'

'To be honest,' she said, pushing Iván's document case
out of the way and leading him into the kitchen, 'I don't
really care what it is. I'm going out of my mind. I've
never had the days stretching emptily ahead like this.'

'Sounds like heaven to me,' said Daniel.

'Please sit down. I'll just boil the kettle.'

'Nice radio.' He turned on her new radio-cassette. She'd been spending money like water to pass the lonely hours. Radio Two blared out a noisy rock tune. 'Terrific! Mind if I keep this on a minute?' he said, raising his voice over the noise.

With a smile, she shook her head and reached up for the biscuit tin.

'You know, you've got a fabulous figure,' shouted Daniel.

The radio snapped off.

'And it belongs to me,' said Iván's voice in the sudden silence, dangerously low, dangerously husky.

Rachel whirled around. Daniel had half risen, only to be pressed down by Iván's hand on his shoulder. Probably Daniel was stronger, but there was such rage in Iván's eyes that he was wisely not putting such a possibility to the test.

'Iván, Daniel was...'

He interrupted Rachel's explanation. 'Now, since you are no longer on duty, Daniel,' said Iván, with silk running through the threat in his voice, 'I suggest you spend the next few hours looking for a new job. This one is about as safe as walking blindfold across a motorway. There's no knowing *what* might happen!'

'Oh, no,' groaned Rachel. 'That isn't fair, Iván. He only came in because I asked him. You see...'

'That,' said Iván in his butter-soft tones, 'is between us and will be dealt with as soon as I've finished with golden boy. Take your Armani shoulders elsewhere, Daniel. I'm sure there are plenty of other bored housewives whose husbands won't object if you amuse them in their absence.' His hand lifted in an unhurried movement, his eyebrow quirked in an unspoken order, and Daniel rose.

'I don't have to go,' he said defiantly.

Iván's eyes chilled. 'Make my day, defy me,' he grated through clenched teeth.

'Daniel! Please go!' cried Rachel, terrified at the violence of Iván's threat.

'OK. But she invited me! I've done nothing wrong!' flung Daniel over his retreating shoulder.

'No. I came home,' shot Iván after him. 'Well, Rachel?'

'I was bored,' she said sulkily. 'Daniel said...'

'I'm not interested. Bored, eh?'

Rachel gulped in fear. 'Why don't you shout like normal men instead of menacing me with softness?' she cried shakily. She took one look at Iván's face and turned tail, running for her old bedroom. But he caught up with her, swung her around and slammed her against the kitchen wall.

'Has that overgrown toy boy made love to you?' he muttered.

'No!' His eyes scared her. They had no depth at all.

'If I thought for one moment that you had been unfaithful to me, I would thrash you and throw you into the river,' he whispered.

'I swear I haven't!' cried Rachel frantically. 'Oh, why are you so cruel to me?'

'I'm hoping it's for the same reason you are cruel to me,' he answered obliquely. 'But at the moment I can't be sure and so I can't take the risk.'

To her relief, he let her go and she moved warily around the kitchen table, rubbing her wrists.

'I'm sorry you were bored,' he continued with menace. 'We must do something about that. Perhaps I should have started as I meant to go on.'

He kept an eye on her as he dialled a number. 'Cancel all my engagements for the next few days,' he said softly. He listened, laughed wickedly, and placed the receiver gently back in its cradle.

Rachel gulped. 'I was thinking about a job,' she said hurriedly. 'A part-time one, to keep me busy. That's why Daniel came in, to offer advice.'

The carved mouth parted in a sigh of irritation. 'You should turn to me when you need advice. I have the perfect answer to your boredom!'

'Oh.' She ran her tongue over suddenly dry lips. 'What's that, then?' Stupid, stupid, stupid! *Why* had she said that?

Before she could move away, Iván had lunged across the table and caught her hand in a relentless grip, pulling her around and jerking her against his body. 'This,' he said, just before his mouth crushed hers. It was no use trying to escape, try as she might. The table edged into her back and Iván's arms held her hard against his un-yielding chest.

'Stop it! Stop it!' she cried, tearing her mouth away and arching backwards. 'You said...'

Iván gave a mocking laugh. 'I know. We'll find out which of us breaks first, shall we?'

'It won't be me! I can't bear being assaulted.'

'Who said anything about assault?'

Calmly, he picked her up and carried her wriggling body into his bedroom, where he slammed the door with his foot and set her down, holding her fast against his powerful body with one arm while he locked the door firmly and threw the key into the corner of the room.

Iván's free hand skimmed over her spine and she steeled herself to the sensation that ran with it. He laughed again and carried her to the bed.

'A little music, I think,' he murmured, turning on the stereo.

'Corny. That won't make me love you,' she said scornfully.

'I'm not expecting love. Wild abandon will do,' he said huskily.

'Huh!'

Iván pressed a switch by the bed, and the curtains slid silently across the window.

'Neat,' she said, with forced interest. 'I've been drawing them by hand all this time. Will you be long? There's a programme on Open University this morning that I want to watch.'

The black eyes glittered. 'I suggest you forget any arrangements you have for the next twenty-four hours,' he said.

'You *are* an optimist, aren't you?' she said caustically.

'Experienced,' he amended, beginning to run a hand over her inert body.

Rachel remained as still as possible, not fighting him at all. She was a person who could only be won by romance, not by the kind of approach Iván was adopting.

The love song ended. Before the next one began, there was silence, apart from their breathing: Rachel's a carefully controlled and studied calm, Iván's quick and shallow. Then she became aware of the sound and the feel of his hands, moving over the material of her blouse, rustling it gently, warming the skin of her shoulders with his light, rhythmical touch. His fingers strayed to the neck of her shirt, slid inside and ventured to the swell of her breast. Rachel willed herself not to respond, not to hold her breath, but looked around the room in resigned boredom. The fingers withdrew.

'Damn you, Rachel,' he breathed. There was no triumph in her eyes as he swung his legs to the side of the bed, only a terrible misery. 'I thought you loved me,' he said woodenly.

'Oh?'

He looked back over his shoulder. 'Don't you?'

'What does it look like?' she asked coldly.

'That,' he said, getting up, 'is a little inconvenient.'

'You only need me to be charming in front of the court when Anna's case comes up,' she said, going over to the dressing-table and tidying her ravaged appearance with enormous care. 'And of course I have to put on a show in public.'

'Yes. What more could I possibly need?' he said cynically. 'It looks as if that house in Lewes will be too large for the three of us. I imagine you don't want me to father your children.'

Rachel almost stopped with her hand in mid-air as it rose to neaten her hair, but willed it on, astonished that this needed so much concentration of effort.

'I'd prefer it if you didn't,' she said stiffly.

'Then we must find something else to keep you occupied,' he said. 'Entertaining blond giants who admire your body is not very wise. I find I'm very jealous of others attempting to take what I haven't yet savoured. Perhaps we ought to go away for a holiday.'

'No!' They'd be thrown together too much. When he had spoken of fathering her children, it had nearly broken her up at the pity of it all. Being near him, day after day, might make her weaken.

'Then we may as well use the free time that's suddenly on our hands and visit Anna. I'm damned if I'm going to rescind my call to cancel my appointments. It would be too humiliating.'

'Oh, of course. We mustn't humiliate the great Iván Posada, must we?' mocked Rachel. 'The face that he presents to the world must always show infallibility, never defeat. It mustn't be said of him that his wife can't bear him to come near her!'

'By God, you've got a steel tip to your tongue nowadays,' he breathed.

'Really? I wonder who I got that from?' she said coldly.

Muttering under his breath, Iván reached for the phone and contacted Diana. 'Unless there's a problem, Diana's going over to collect Anna straight away,' he said eventually. 'Apparently the kiddie has been waiting to see us and driving Emily nuts. She'll be glad to get her off her hands for a while. Get your things. We'll drive down to Brighton immediately.'

At least it would make a change. And she could enjoy herself a little in Anna's company. The drive wasn't much fun, though. An uneasy silence filled the car interior with tension. Iván was the first to break it.

'Rachel, this is going to be a little difficult for both of us,' he said with a worried frown as they cleared Marble Arch.

'I know what's expected of me,' she said, stony-faced.

'Good.' There was the suspicion of a break in his voice.

Rachel stared openly at his stern mouth and hard jaw, and then fixed her gaze ahead. She had to work herself into a wifely role for Anna's sake—and to fool Diana.

She needn't have bothered. Anna was so excited, her huge dark eyes alight with happiness, the black plaits bobbing wildly as she danced around in glee, that Rachel could have worn a Hallowe'en mask and the little girl would hardly have noticed. Not so Diana.

'Anna, stop hugging everyone's knees and let your father and Rachel come inside,' she said. 'You're looking very pretty, Rachel. And a lot thinner.'

Rachel had piled her hair on top of her head and dressed for the country in a warm wool jacket, sweater and cords. The turquoise colours in her outfit went some way to alleviating her pallor, but there was a luminous quality about her face that hadn't been there before.

Diana's rooms were elegance themselves, extending over the ground floor of a huge Regency building, with high ceilings and huge bow windows that looked on to a colonnaded Regency square.

'This is beautiful,' cried Rachel in surprise.

'Well, thank you,' said Diana. 'Would you like to look around? Iván, you can catch up on news with Anna. She's dying to drop hints about birthday presents, I think. Rachel, you must see my conservatory, it's the pride of my life.'

Glad to be out of Iván's intimidating presence, Rachel followed Diana, admiring the clean, classical lines of the spacious rooms, and, having shed her jacket in Diana's gold and white bedroom, pushed up the sleeves of her sweater, sweltering in the heated conservatory.

'You have really lost weight,' said Diana critically. 'And why is Iván so miserable?'

'I—I don't know what you mean,' said Rachel, flushing. 'My, it's hot in here, isn't it?'

'These are all sub-tropical plants,' said Diana, glancing around with satisfaction at the jungle, then back at Rachel. 'You love him, he loves you. So what's the problem?'

Rachel's jaw had dropped open. 'Are you trying to be funny?' she asked sharply. 'I know you must hate me...'

'Hate? My dear girl, I love Iván far too much to hate you. If you're what he wants,' her thin shoulders shrugged, 'then that's what I want for him, too. But I've seen that man from the early days when I was a young bride. I know when he's being ripped apart by hungry wolves inside. He ought to be shattered with love, satiated with happiness, and all the vibes I get from you two are sheathed in ice.'

Leaning back against the doorway, Rachel shut her eyes. 'You must know that Iván only married me to get custody of Anna and to spite Tony,' she began tonelessly.

'What?' came Diana's incredulous cry. 'Nothing of the kind! His brain has been scattered in all directions because he loves you so much!'

'Please...' begged Rachel in pain, her eyes huge.

'You stupid pair! You need your heads banging together!' snapped Diana. 'That man loves you. He told me in such humble, wondering, tender words that I cried for him. Whatever is blocking communication between you, get it going! He's a prize idiot. He's spent so much of his life learning to hide his feelings... Oh, Rachel, he's lived in a minefield of lies and deceit all his life. Imagine what it must have been like to be brutally beaten on your grandfather's orders, at his father's funeral! That's when I stopped hating and resenting the hold he and his mother had over Philip and started loving him and pitying, too. I saw that magnificent, stupid pride of his and the way he struggled to his feet, took his mother's arm and *still* walked to Philip's graveside, bruised and battered as he was. No one touched him; they didn't dare, he was utterly invincible from then on. Outside, not inside. He's suffered every wound imaginable since then. Don't freeze him out, or you'll lose the best man you'll ever get, Rachel Posada! Your marriage will turn sour...'

'It already has!' she wailed. 'He doesn't love me! He won't give an inch!'

'Damned pride! Damned mother!' growled Diana angrily. 'Do you want me to keep Anna here while you two go off and sort yourselves out?' she suggested. 'Because if you don't, I'm going to sit you both down and lecture you. I'm not wrong, am I? You do love him?'

'I do, I don't...yes. No... It's just that... I can't bear to expose myself to his cruelty. I...yes, I love him so much that if he was really hurtful, I'd feel suicidal.'

'Iván has had far too many disappointments in life and far too little love for you to hold back,' said Diana. 'Believe me. I think he loves you so much that—like you—he daren't risk rejection because that would destroy him for ever. You *are* two of a kind, aren't you?' she smiled.

Iván had said that once. She could remain distant, growing colder with the years in self-protection. He would behave in exactly the same way, till the barriers between them were impassable. Or...she could take a gamble that Diana was right.

'Isn't he worth the risk?' probed Diana.

'I'm afraid,' she breathed.

'So's he. And desperately unhappy. Do you like making him miserable?'

'No! I—I'll find a way,' said Rachel. 'I——'

'*Rakle!* Come *on*! Daddy's doin' our secret.' Anna's bellow rang down the marble-floored corridor.

Rachel raised brimming eyes to Diana. 'Why...' The ache in the back of her throat prevented her from continuing.

'Because I love and admire him,' said Diana gently. 'Like everyone who gets under that thick defence and finds out what he's like. And because somebody in this damned family had better be happy. Go on. Straighten your marriage out.'

Rachel nodded. There was this terrible wall of pride and coldness between them, and she wasn't sure if she could fight her way through it, past Iván's lifetime of defences. At the door of the kitchen, she paused. He

was there, head bent, intently covering a sheet of paper
with thick crayon.

You fool, Iván Lutero Posada! A man as old and wise
and experienced as you, afraid to trust your judgement.
I *told* you . . . Rachel's heart dropped to her boots. She'd
also implied that she didn't, that she hated him. Tenderly, her eyes moved slowly over his tense face. He knew
she was there and was studiously ignoring her. She must
begin.

Rachel slid into a seat beside him and he looked up
with a frown. 'I'm told that if I cover this thickly enough,
I'll see a miracle,' he said abruptly. 'Apparently it's
something amazing you do with Anna.'

'Let me help,' said Rachel casually, stretching her
hands towards a stubby crayon. Iván flinched as her arm
brushed his hand. 'Every bit must be covered in wax,'
she added emotionally, beginning to fill in the corner.

'You do it,' he said, pushing back his chair.

'No, Daddy! You, too! Or Rakle won't give you the
surprise!

His lip momentarily lost its tight line and was drawn
in under his sharp white teeth. It showed white when he
released it, then blood-red.

Rachel was tantalisingly aware of his tense body, and
of Diana watching sympathetically. Deliberately she tilted
her head on one side so that her fragrant hair brushed
his temple. He leaned away.

'It's done,' he said with evident relief.

Rachel looked at Diana despairingly, but she gave an
encouraging smile.

'Anna, you'd all better go now, or you'll never have
time to try out your secret and show Daddy that miracle,'
she said. 'I've arranged, by the way, for Anna to stay
the night. Emily has found a certain *enfant* a little beyond
her. She's more and more unable to cope. Anna,

it would be nice if Daddy and Rachel stayed the night, too, wouldn't it?'

Oh, you darling, thought Rachel.

'No!' shot Iván.

'Yes, that would be lovely,' said Rachel calmly. 'Thank you, Diana. Shall we go, Iván?'

Biting back any comment and accompanied by a hopeful Rachel and an exuberant Anna, a very puzzled Iván made his way to the car and drove in grim silence to a small hamlet on the outskirts of Lewes. Anna had demanded to be taken to a pond. She was mad about ponds.

Oblivious of her father's mood, she chattered to him and Rachel, dancing on ahead when they parked, clutching three pieces of heavily crayoned paper. There was a feel of winter about the air: a gloom and greyness, and a bleak quiet that hung over the downland and permeated the wet, earthy smell of decaying leaves under their feet. Rachel felt that something momentous was about to happen. It either meant that she would find Diana was wrong, and she was about to learn just how scathing Iván could be to people who went too far, or that all the tiny glimpses of a different Iván could really add up into one, loving man, too injured to create his own chances for love and needing the first terrifying step of commitment to come from someone else.

'Do it, do it! Please!' Anna cavorted about Rachel in a mad jig.

'Come on then, Scrub,' she laughed, sitting on the wet grass by the water.

Iván slipped off his anorak and motioned for her to rise, settling it under her without comment. She mumbled her thanks somewhat incoherently, giving her attention to the paper, folding each piece.

'Look! Boats!' cried Anna proudly, showing them to him.

'So they are,' he smiled wanly.

On an impulse, Rachel pulled out the pins in her hair, allowing it to run free through her fingers in a wickedly sexy gesture, but she couldn't look at him. All she knew was that her heart was thudding like a piston and her mouth was so dry she had to keep moistening her lips to speak at all.

They watched as Anna placed the boats on the water and blew at them gently, sending them in different directions.

'She knows paper gets soggy,' said Rachel, in the general direction of Iván's knees. 'And that the crayon makes them waterproof. Usually, on the farm, we put sprigs of plants in the boats as people.'

'Plants?' He sat down next to her in astonishment.

'Herbs. I got the idea from a children's programme I used to watch. There's Basil, Rosemary, Parsley—she's learning all their names.'

'How can bits of herbs be people?' he frowned.

'When you're that age, anything is possible, if you believe it passionately enough,' she answered softly, lifting her gentle face to him. 'If you feel deeply. Like discovering someone loves you after all, even when you'd given up hope.'

Iván gazed down at her, his face puzzled. A huge tear had appeared in the corner of each one of her beautiful, big, liquid-brown eyes.

His thumb tilted her chin, his finger reaching for each tear.

'Who are you crying for?' he asked gently.

'Us,' she croaked.

'But there's no need,' he whispered. 'The spell is broken, as the good fairy used to say. Isn't it?'

Unable to speak, she nodded fiercely, trying to focus on Anna, learning how to make the boats by unfolding and refolding the paper repeatedly. Through her tears and rapidly fluttering lashes, she could tell that Iván was very upset. He buried his head in her shoulder and held her so tightly that she could hardly breathe.

'Thank God I can hold you at last!' he whispered. 'I thought you'd never relent. I *said* I'd never marry without love, but you refused to respond to that.'

'I didn't think you meant yourself,' wailed Rachel.

'Who else? I nearly backed out from marrying you, I had such doubts for your sake. Then when I couldn't reach you through sex...'

'You could have reached me through love,' she said.

'I—I thought I could best tell you through love-making how tenderly I felt. I didn't dare to risk... Oh, God! Forgive me, and understand that I learnt too early in life never to trust anyone completely. You see, when you refused me, I was bewildered. My life began to hurtle into hell once more.'

'Sex without love isn't my scene.'

'I know,' he said humbly. 'I've been a fool. You deserve a better man than me.'

'Yes,' said Rachel, dead-pan. 'But I love you, so I suppose I'll have to make do.' She betrayed her words with a quirk at the corner of her mouth.

'Don't tease me. I'm very tender. I've only just begun to learn how to love and how to trust. Lucky for you, I'm a fast learner!' he declared with a heart-stopping grin.

'Oh, Iván!' How silly of her to cry!

'Hush, you're tearing me apart with your tears. You'll have me howling in a moment, my darling, and what will that do to my Rambo image?'

She grinned, her mouth going through some odd, trembling contortions to achieve that grin. 'Never Rambo,' she said. 'Who are you kidding? I think, under that lacquered surface, you're Rupert Bear.'

Iván kissed every salt drop he could find on her face, and some he couldn't, his tongue sinuously sliding up her face.

'My mascara...'

'Oh, very female,' he murmured. 'It hasn't run. If it had, I'd be cleaning that up, too.'

His hands ravelled her hair, threading in wild sweeps. 'I have to stop touching you,' he muttered. 'Anna is a little young to witness what I have in mind.'

She smiled, content to wait. For the rest of that afternoon, they lost themselves in Anna's game of Let's Pretend, finding sticks to represent themselves, setting them in the boats and creating stories. Finally, at Iván's insistence—not very hotly contested—two of the sticks got married and the other was the bridesmaid.

When they arrived at Diana's, it wasn't necessary for any words to be said. She knew immediately from the ridiculously romantic expressions on Iván and Rachel's faces that they had found each other at last.

Rachel stood at the foot of Anna's bed later that night, watching the child sleeping. Iván's secure arm was around Rachel's waist, her head was on his shoulder.

'Now our turn, my darling,' he murmured, feathering a kiss on her temple.

'It's early! Only nine o'clock!' she protested weakly.

'I always longed for a wife who could tell the time,' he said with a laugh.

'Iván... Promise me something,' she said hesitantly.

'Anything.'

'If we win the custody case for Anna, don't shut Emily out. She's devoted her life to your child.'

'I know. I'll talk to her. The way I feel, soft and squishy, loving everyone, I'm in danger of befriending Jaws, let alone my half-sister. And Tony. After all, they fought me because I fought them. We'll come to some arrangement, I give you my word. The only thing that bothers me is that I'm likely to lose my job.'

'Iván! Why?'

'I told you, I feel stupidly warm towards my fellow man. That's not the best attitude for a satirist to take! But who cares, at this moment?'

His palms captured her jaw, and pulsing nerves took over her brain as his lips poised fractionally over her mouth, every unhappy moment of her brief marriage was forgotten in the knowledge that he could be tender, he could care and that she loved him so wildly that he was driving her mad with this tension.

'Why don't you kiss me?' she implored.

He growled in his throat, his eyes smiling and wanting at the same time. 'If I do,' he breathed, fanning her face with teasing breath, 'I shan't be able to stop. I'm ravenous, my darling. Utterly ravenous.' He finished on another growl, visibly shaking in the effort to keep control until she granted him permission to appease their hunger.

Rachel couldn't speak for wanting him. But it was in her head, as well as her body; nothing else mattered but to make that final unbreakable liaison, where she and Iván shared everything with each other, trusting and letting go.

She raised soft, doe-brown eyes to him, and reached forwards with her mouth. Tenderly he took it, lightly tracing its outline with the tip of his tongue first, and then brushing it gently with his firm, dry lips. Her tongue slid out and explored his mouth, while he groaned in pleasure, his eyes half-shut in ecstasy.

Iván drew her from the room and into their own, still bending his dark head, plundering and raiding her mouth. Without a word to each other their hasty fingers struggled with zips and buttons, straps and belts until they were both naked and untouching, apart from their hungry mouths.

The ripples were coursing steadily through her body now, pooling in her feet, wave upon wave of them, till she swayed with the raw, aching desire.

Iván stood back and his hot eyes raked her body, closing for brief moments as he fought to stay sane. Rachel was nearly out of her mind, her breathing raising her ribcage and thrusting her breasts at him, the very action tightening the cherry peaks into hard little buds, even though he wasn't even touching her.

Reverently he knelt and wrapped his arms around her waist, muttering something incoherent. She slid to the floor and they held each other. Rachel began to stroke the harsh lines of his face, wondering why he was so agonised.

Then she had smoothed the lines away. Iván smiled gently at her and snatched at her fingers with sharp teeth.

'I'm not sure whether to run away from you or stay,' he said.

'Why would you want to run away?'

'You terrify me. I could almost commit murder for you, do you know that? And losing control is not something I like. It's taken me too long to learn how to contain my feelings.'

'You mustn't do that with me.' Her fingers curled around his ear, teasingly.

'Aaah, don't do that!' he groaned. 'It's just as well for you that I have controlled myself. I don't think you or Daniel knew how close I was to throwing him through my plate-glass windows and taking that smug, sexy smile off his handsome face.'

'Why, Mr Posada! Jealous?' Her eyes laughed at him in delight.

'Can't you see?' he asked, showing her the side of his face. 'Aren't I a deep shade of emerald-green?'

She kissed along the high bone and tasted his scar with her tongue. Iván let out a long breath and grabbed her hair, pulling back her head and laying her out on the floor at the same time. The whole wonderful length of his body lay on her: hard corded muscles in his back, big muscular shoulders... Her hands drew sensitising paths over the soft skin, as Iván watched her face and the emotions that played there. She could just about reach down to the curve of his waist and the swell of his hipbone, her fingers delighting in the strength and power that lay in her arms.

'I love you, Rachel. Love, love, love you.'

He seemed to be waiting. His deep chest rounded with the hammering of his heart, pulses quivered in his throat and the ragged breathing in her ear and the hardness against her body told her how painful his wait was proving to be.

'I love you, too. Will you make love to me?' she asked simply.

'I thought you'd never ask,' he growled.

Rachel reached out a hand and touched the wig pegs in Anna's bedroom, one by one. Over the years, they had held her bags of toys, school satchels, school-tie, roller-skates, and ski-boots.

In that time, with Diana's help, the Latimer family had eventually become reconciled with the newly gentle Iván, so much so that Tony had become godfather to Rachel and Iván's two sons, and an outrageously indulgent uncle to Emily's two adopted daughters. The distant cousin who claimed the farm had no wish to move from his own comfortable house, and so Tony, Mike and Emily stayed on as caretakers. Tony eventually married and had a son of his own, too. And because the absentee owner of Latimer farm was a bachelor, Tony's heir would eventually inherit it.

'The hat, the hat, you forget it!'

Rachel turned to smile at Teresa, and lifted the bridal veil from the wooden peg.

'You fix it, Teresa,' she said, and watched the vibrant, excitable woman arranging the cluster of wild poppies in Anna's blue-black hair. The reflections of Iván's daughter and his mother looked back at her with Iván's eyes, his cheekbones, his beauty, and she knew her eyes were bright with unshed tears.

There was a tap on the door, and Iván walked in, tall, so utterly handsome that Rachel's breath caught in her throat at the sight of him.

'Don't cry, Rachel,' he said gently. 'Or I will, too, and then *everyone* will know I'm soft to the core.'

'Mmm.' She slid into his arms, her gold watered-silk ensemble a perfect complement to his morning-suit. 'We mustn't let that happen, must we? Think of the headlines. Famous investigative author sobs at daughter's wedding.'

He grinned, his slashing white, dazzling grin that melted her heart as always and, at that moment, Anna rose from the dressing-table and turned to them all.

Iván's black eyes turned to dark treacle. 'How beautiful you are,' he whispered, embracing her with tender care. 'Whose idea was it to keep you wild with the poppies?'

'Mine,' laughed Teresa. 'Like you and me, she's not the conventional sort.'

'Heaven help her husband,' grinned Iván.

'He can't wait,' answered Anna with a laugh.

'Are we all ready?' he asked Rachel. 'I left two elegant young men downstairs, cooling their heels. They seemed vaguely familiar.'

'Ah! My handsome grandsons!' Teresa rushed from the room.

'Elegant, did you say? This, I've got to see,' grinned Anna, following.

'I love you, my darling,' said Iván, touching Rachel's thick pile of hair in wonder.

'Then kiss me,' she whispered.

'I thought you'd never ask,' he smiled.

Harlequin Presents

Coming Next Month

ATTRACTIVE, SPACE SAVING BOOK RACK

Display your most prized novels on this handsome and sturdy book rack. The hand-rubbed walnut finish will blend into your library decor with quiet elegance, providing a practical organizer for your favorite hard-or soft-covered books.

Only $9.95

Approximately 16" x 8" when assembled

Assembles in seconds!

To order, rush your name, address and zip code, along with a check or money order for $10.70* ($9.95 plus 75¢ postage and handling) payable to *Harlequin Reader Service*:

> Harlequin Reader Service
> Book Rack Offer
> 901 Fuhrmann Blvd.
> P.O. Box 1396
> Buffalo, NY 14269-1396
>
> *Offer not available in Canada.*

BKR-1A

*New York and Iowa residents add appropriate sales tax.

Harlequin Historicals

Step into a world of pulsing adventure, gripping emotion and lush sensuality with these evocative love stories penned by today's best-selling authors in the highest romantic tradition. Pursuing their passionate dreams against a backdrop of the past's most colorful and dramatic moments, our vibrant heroines and dashing heroes will make history come alive for you.

Watch for two new Harlequin Historicals each month, available wherever Harlequin books are sold. History was never so much fun—you won't want to miss a single moment!